OF BOOKS AND BONES

A BRIGHTON VILLAGE COZY MYSTERY
NOVELLA

SYLVIE KURTZ

Iris Ink

ALSO BY SYLVIE KURTZ

Other

A Little Christmas Magic, a Holiday Romance

Broken Wings, a Time Travel Romance

Silver Shadows, a Paranormal Romance

Ms. Longshot, It Girls Book 4

For my readers

Thank you for choosing to spend time with my stories.

1
_____

When my sister-in-law, Page Hamlin, who owned The Purple Page Bookshop, got an idea into her head, it usually led to trouble.

She'd closed the bookstore an hour early on this Sunday afternoon to prepare for the construction work that would start in the morning. She was expanding her bookstore into the empty Chic Boutique space next door. Given this was Brighton, New Hampshire, where people were more apt to wear fleece and flannel than silk or sequins, the closure last September didn't come as a surprise. What did was that it had lasted so long.

Midnight came and went. We'd created an area for the workers, giving them privacy with the bookcases while keeping the book browsers safe from falling debris by blocking access to the construction zone.

Page and I were dizzy with fatigue, not to mention over-chocolated. Page's hair had gone from tidy tawny ponytail to a witch frizz. Dust streaked her cheeks, her "I'm with the Banned" T-shirt and her skirt. And she'd broken two of her pumpkin-decorated nails. I probably didn't look any better. I felt every muscle in my body and longed for a hot shower and bed.

Page pushed a package of mint Tim Tams my way along the oak floorboards as we sat, appreciating our hard work.

"One more for the road, Ellie?" Page asked.

"Ugh." I pressed a hand over my aching stomach. "I don't think so."

"This would've been easier with Harlan's help," Page said with a tsk.

"You know your brother." I hiked a shoulder, inevitable resentment crawling up my throat uninvited. "He took Lander's shift today because Lander gave him some sort of sob story."

I loved Harlan. We'd been married forever. We'd raised three children together and made a great team. But sometimes, he drove me crazy with his habit of always helping strangers first. He took the "Serve and Protect" motto of the Brighton PD too much to heart. I got that Brighton wasn't crawling with cops to take up the slack. Harlan was in charge and felt he had to fill the voids himself. But still. You'd think that his own family would at least make the top three of the to-help list. At least he'd recently hired a new officer, so that was progress.

Page, hands at heart level, clapped in quick succession. "I can't wait to open the café."

"Do you think Maeve Carpenter will be upset about the competition?"

Page dismissed my question with a wave of her hand and a *pfft*. "A, her bakery's at the other end of Main Street. And B, I'm not going to offer the same fare. Definitely not as fancy."

"Um," I grumbled.

"Don't *um* me, Ellie. I'm going to keep it simple."

I snorted. "Like you did when Lisa Gardner came for a signing."

"Well..."

"You made twenty kinds of brownies."

"She likes brownies, and I didn't know what kind she liked best."

"She would have liked any *one* kind."

"She loved the gun-shaped ones." Page smiled at the memory.

"Not the point, Page."

Page stared at the right-hand wall as if she could already see the arch and through it the café with its tables and chairs and its glass case filled with goodies. "I'm just going to offer a couple kinds of cookies and muffins. Maybe a breakfast sandwich and a couple of lunch sandwiches. Coffee and tea. Maybe hot chocolate. Soup in winter would be good."

Already her plan was mushrooming out of control. "Which will morph into a dozen different things because you hate to disappoint anyone. Then you'll complain you're overwhelmed."

"I'm going to hire a manager," Page said, running her hands down the gauzy folds of her amethyst skirt.

"That is a *great* idea." She needed someone to keep her wild ideas in check.

"I'll be right back." Page scrambled up and headed toward the restroom.

Being around Page for any length of time tended to make me lose sight of common sense and act like a kid. I should have insisted on a proper meal. But this had been fun. A nice diversion from my not-so-pleasant thoughts about my future.

"Look what I found!" Page giggled like a schoolgirl when she came back. She struggled to lift a sledgehammer. She swung it around with barely any control. Where had it even come from?

I moved out of range. "I think you should put that down before you hurt someone, i.e., me."

Her eyes blazed with what I recognized as a bad idea. "Let's do it."

"Do what?"

She twisted like a manic jewelry box ballerina toward the wall. "Crack a hole in the wall."

Yep, a really bad idea. I reached for the hammer, but she wobbled out of reach. "Isn't that why you're paying Aaron the big bucks?"

"Ah, come on, Ellie. It'll be fun. We'll inaugurate the new space. I want to show you what I want to do."

"I can see the outline of the arch."

"Inside." She lifted the hammer again, then almost dropped it on her foot. "Forgot," she said, speed walking like a duck, dragging the hammer, toward the checkout counter where she picked up her reading glasses. "Safety first!"

"Don't you have a key?"

Eyes scrunched, she aimed the wobbly hammer at the wall. "This is going to be way more fun."

She lifted the hammer over her head and took a few steps backward with the weight of it.

"What if it's a retaining wall?" I asked, knowing Page well enough to understand that trying to stop her would just create more problems.

"Aaron said this was the area he was going to open up." With the hammer, she traced the pencil line on the wall, showing the placement of the arch. Then with a huff and a heave, she loosed the hammer at the wall. Plaster, drywall and wood splinters flew.

She pushed her glasses up her nose. "Good thing I was wearing these."

"Reading glasses are not meant as construction-area eye protection."

She swung again and this time hit something that didn't sound like any kind of wall material. When the plaster stopped falling, a piece of black nylon webbing snaked through and hung like a noose.

"Looks like he was wrong," I said, stepping closer. "There's something in there."

Page stuck her head in the hole in the wall. "I don't see any weight-bearing beams or anything. It just looks like some sort of bag. Like luggage or something." She stuck a hand out. "Get me a flashlight."

"Be careful." This building was old. Who knew what kind of germs and bugs lived there. "And, no, I won't get you a flashlight. I think we should go home."

She tugged on the handle, but the bag refused to move. "Give me a hand with this."

"Why don't we leave it for the workers?"

She turned on me, eyes feverish. She loved a good mystery and had always wanted to live one. "What if it's a treasure? You know this area has a long and checkered history, don't you?"

I'd heard local legends about the robber barons, the magical angel and the twisted trees. All of them seemed more about luring tourists into the Brighton fantasy than actual fact. "You forget, I'm a newbie. I've only been around for thirty years."

Page snort-laughed. "Newbie. A baby Brightonian. Just a widdle baby Brightonian."

Okay, that was enough. I tried to lead Page away from the wall. She obviously needed rest. "Let's look at it in the morning."

"Nooooo!" she cried like an overtired child about to have a tantrum and kept yanking on the handles until a chunk of wall fell away. The bag, the size of an army duffel, popped out, knocking Page over. She landed on the floor on her rump with a dull plop. I rushed over to help her.

"What do you think's in there?" Page asked, scrambling into a crouch beside the bag. "Money? Bonds? Oooh, jewelry? Do you think it's finders keepers? I mean, it's in the wall, so technically it could be mine just as well as Lillian's, right?"

Dust grayed the black heavy-duty canvas of the bag. It reminded me of Harlan's duffel bag when he and Lander went on camping trips to supposedly fish. "How did all that even fit in the narrow wall?"

"It's heavy," Page said, reaching for the zipper.

I placed a hand over hers. I had a bad feeling. "I think we should wait."

"I don't." With a flourish of hand, she yanked on the zipper. White powder puffed out, filled my nostrils, made them burn. The sides of the bag sagged, exposing something dirty beige, speckled with bright red dots. My stomach heaved, churning all those Halloween M&Ms and mint Tim Tams into a sour mash.

Page reached inside but I grabbed her wrist. Blood drained from my face. I was going to be sick. "Don't. You don't know what that powder is. For all we know we've just been poisoned."

"Come on, Ellie! Stop being such a downer."

I squeezed her wrist tight, my heart racing faster than if I'd run a marathon. "We need to call Harlan."

She tried to tug free of my grasp, but I held on firm. "He couldn't bother to help, so why should he get to have fun?"

I looked Page straight in the eyes, so she would see my dread. "I think these are bones."

2

Harlan arrived at the bookshop ten minutes later, Owen McGill, his new officer, in tow. Harlan looked haggard after his over-twelve-hour shift that would now extend indefinitely. We were waiting for the crime scene van to arrive to collect the evidence for the lab to analyze.

Owen nodded at me to acknowledge my presence. "Ma'am."

"Oh, for heaven's sake, Owen. You're dating our daughter. Call me Ellie."

His cheeks turned apple red, and he shuffled his feet. "Yes, ma'a—uh, Ellie."

Owen and our middle child, Everly, had reconnected on one of his holiday trips back home. After deciding he wouldn't make a good lawyer, he'd gone into law enforcement. Fresh out of the academy, he'd answered Brighton's call for manpower—and started dating Evie. Something I still had in the let's-see-how-this-works-out department.

Harlan had insisted Page go home, sending Owen along with her to make sure she did. I'd given Owen my car keys so he wouldn't be stranded at Page's.

"Did you touch anything?" Harlan crouched beside the duffel, examining the contents. He'd always looked good in a uniform. The navy shirt still fit nicely on those broad shoulders and the navy pants hugged his narrow waist. That's how we'd met—when my college roommate and I had ventured from Boston to Brighton for a Fall Festival and broken down on the side of the road in the middle of nowhere. He was a rookie then, just starting out as a patrol officer.

"Of course, I didn't touch anything!" How many hours had we sat around the kitchen table, talking about his days and his cases and procedures? He could do that because he knew I was discreet and could hold on to a confidence.

"Page?" he asked.

"Just the zipper. The bag did fall on top of her."

He nodded. "Okay."

He shifted his long body to a different angle, crabbing to get a better look. "What possessed you to play construction?"

"Well, someone didn't show up to help, so you know how your sister gets..."

His gaze caught mine and he lifted a brow. "You're the logical one. You should've kept her in check."

"You obviously don't spend enough time with family to know your sister."

He grumbled. "Not the time for this, Ellie."

"It never is."

"Ellie..."

I waved a hand. "If it's a body, why doesn't it stink?"

"Probably lime. And time."

"That white powder is lime?"

He nodded but didn't offer more.

"How old do you think these bones are?" I asked.

"The building is seventy-five years old. So that's the outer edge." He chucked a chin toward the bag. "Those sequins aren't that old."

They sparkled in the light of the shop, somehow still looking mostly new. "Plastic lives forever."

He muttered something I couldn't hear.

"Do you think it's a whole skeleton?" I asked.

"Looks like it. It'll make identification easier—at least sex, age and height."

The bones had looked human to me, but I wasn't an anthropologist, and many animal bones could look like human bones. "You're sure it's human?"

"Don't know many animals that wear sequins."

True enough. Sequins made the victim most likely female.

Harlan went to his patrol car and came back with a camera. I leaned against a bookcase and watched him work. He was focused, methodical and left no space unexamined by his or his camera's eye. I'd always liked watching him work. His cool and composed demeanor had calmed me back when we'd met, and I was a mess. With Harlan around, I'd felt safe, secure.

"Do you have any unsolved missing people cases that would fit these bones?" I asked, working through the files of my memories for some of his cold cases.

"Several."

A sore point with him. The boy who'd disappeared into the woods and was never found. The girl who'd gone missing from a football game and was still missing. The nurse whose car had broken down on the side of the road and was never seen again. But neither the nurse nor the high school girl was likely to have worn sequins when she disappeared.

Brighton didn't see much crime. Most of Harlan's cases over the years had fallen under the domestic and drunk driving category. I knew better than to ask if he thought these bones belonged to one of his missing people. His answer would be, "Won't know till I get the results back from the medical examiner."

He wasn't big on speculating.

One of my skills was my ability to melt into the background and become invisible. So, when the crime scene van arrived, I faded into the bookcases. No one asked me to leave. The place soon buzzed with the sound of flashes, evidence bags crinkling, and voices giving directions.

Growing up, my brother and I used to play a memory game. At any moment, one of us would say, "Close your eyes." Then follow that with questions about the space we occupied. How many people sat along the counter of the diner? How many kids on the playground? What state was that car's license from?

After 9/11, he'd enlisted, even though I'd begged him not to. And he'd come home in a flag-draped coffin. He was my big brother, and I'd adored him. His death left me sometimes feeling like half a ghost.

I swallowed hard, hearing his voice in my head. "Come on, Elize, focus. What are the techs aiming their cameras at?"

All angles of the bag. Black. Canvas. Like a big gym bag. Was that writing on the side? Smudged dirt. No, more like a stain. Blood? Blood would make it murder. Although, really, nobody stuffed themselves in a bag between walls without help.

A bag like a hundred others. But it had a certain male quality to it, didn't it? Most women would've gone for something more colorful, something with a little style. Not this basic black. Which brought me back to a domestic dispute. How often had a woman become some guy's punching bag in these parts? Anger made them strike out and they didn't know their own strength. Then came shame, the need to hide, or at least pretend it was the victim's fault.

How had this woman ended up in the wall separating a boutique with outdated clothes and an overstuffed bookstore? I couldn't think of anyone in a relationship who'd disappeared.

Now the tech aimed his camera at the bones, opening the

bag gently with a gloved hand to get a better view inside. I craned my neck, catching the curve of a skull, the long bones of arms and legs, the bowl of a pelvis. All covered with that white powder. Yep, definitely human. Curled in a fetal position. At the sight, I placed a hand over my aching heart. Had she known fear in her last moments? Pain? Was she calling out for her mother?

A tech called Harlan over, pointing at something I couldn't see at the back of her skull.

Harlan nodded, snapped a few photographs, and backed away so the techs could finish their job.

Then, just as they were getting ready to zip the duffel and place it in a body bag for transport, something flashed in the light. A pendant on a delicate gold chain tangled in the ribs. A round moon cutout with a star charm.

My nerve endings zinged. I knew that pendant. I'd seen it before. But where?

"LET'S GO," Harlan said, wrapping an arm around my shoulders and leading me toward the shop's front door. I loved the feel of his arms around me. How it made me feel safe. Outside, I blinked. The sun had come up and Main Street hummed with activity. Traffic heading toward jobs. Double-parked trucks making deliveries. Sleepy people looking for caffeine. Lookie-loos gawking at the bookshop with its flapping crime scene tape. For all they knew, it was part of Page's Halloween decor.

I could use a pot of coffee. Not that I could fall asleep with all the questions churning in my mind. Who was that woman? How had she ended up wearing sequins and stuffed in a duffel bag between two walls? Why? And where had I seen that necklace before? That question would niggle at me until I had an answer. Once my brain latched on to something, it found it hard to let go until the task was complete or the question answered.

We got home to our little ranch outside of town just as the school bus trundled through the neighborhood. And by ranch, I meant house style, not a place to raise animals, although we'd done our share of guinea pig, dog, cat, chicken, even goat-raising over the years with three kids. All we had left now was a four-year-old mutt of undetermined origin but with some sort of shaggy ancestor. If I wanted to keep my home relatively neat, Stella Luna needed a haircut every six weeks—something I didn't even do for myself.

Stella body-slammed us with all her thirty pounds before we finished crossing the threshold. You'd think she hadn't seen us for a year. Telling her *Off!* didn't work when she'd frothed herself in such a state, becoming a brown-and-white blur with a helicopter tail and a manic tongue. She was supposed to be my dog—a gift to myself after our last child left home. But Harlan was the love of her life.

"I'm going to take the dog out," I said, reaching for the tie-dye harness and pink leash.

"I'm going to grab a couple hours." Harlan headed toward our bedroom at the back of the house. I marveled at how he'd taught himself to sleep on command. I spent way too many restless nights staring at the ceiling, begging my mind to slow down and sleep to find me. Worrying about him. About the kids. About too many things that didn't matter.

"Come on, Stella, let's let him take his nap."

She craned her neck in Harlan's direction and whined.

"Go potty, then you can go nap with him."

As if she understood, she headed for her favorite oak tree, did her business in no time flat—which wasn't usual at all—

then trotted back to the house, tugging on the leash for me to go faster. She turned her nose at the breakfast I offered and waited patiently by our bedroom door for me to open it. With a sigh, I bid her command. "Don't wake him up."

She hopped up at the foot of the bed, where Harlan had flopped still dressed in his uniform, and curled at the V of his legs.

I padded to the kitchen, started a pot of coffee and rummaged through the junk drawer for a pad of paper and a pencil. I needed to get all my thoughts out of my brain. Maybe then it would allow me to rest.

Over the years, I'd become Harlan's sounding board whenever he investigated a case. He'd taught me that solving a case came down to a close examination of details—two pairs of eyes and two points of view were better than one. On the pad, I wrote: Powder. Bones. Black duffel bag. Sequins. Necklace.

By the end of my second cup, I had three pages full of notes, a sour stomach and a growing dread.

I tiptoed to Harlan's office where he kept a copy of the files on the cold cases he couldn't give up. Cold cases he spent way too many weekends going over, hiking the area woods in hopes of finding them.

Seven victims. One murder whose killer he'd identified but couldn't provide enough evidence to stick in court. Six missing, never found.

And with all the woods that surrounded Brighton, Harlan had a lot of ground to cover if he hoped to unearth their last resting place. I should offer to go with him instead of stewing over his absence. At least we'd spend time together. Something I dearly missed.

Harlan was old school. He liked to look at actual paper when he did his thinking on the cold cases. I pulled the two files that seemed the most likely to fit the bones and studied them. Then just because it was that or pace until Harlan woke up, I skimmed through the other files. I discarded the files on the two missing males.

An hour later, I had an uncomfortable inkling as to the identity of the woman in the wall.

3

I jogged from Harlan's office to the bookcase in the living room, scouring the shelves. Not there. I headed for the room our daughters Camden and Everly had shared growing up. On the bottom shelf of their bookcase, I found what I was looking for—Cam's high school yearbooks.

I plopped on the floor and flipped through the pages until I found Cammy's senior class photos. I had a good eye for faces, for details. Someone you wanted to have on your trivia team because my brain hung on to random facts.

I had to go all the way to the Ps before my body went rigid and I gasped involuntarily. Devan Payne. The blond, blue-eyed daughter of the town's bank manager, a bloated man with a mean streak he loved to exercise. Her mother volunteered on all the right boards to impress all the right people.

The last few pages of the yearbook were filled with a tribute to Devan. Teachers had nothing but good things to say about her. After the cheerleader disappeared right in the middle of a football game, there were vigils and months of news coverage.

One minute there, the next gone, never to be seen again.

Every year during the homecoming football game, her

photo was trotted out to keep her top-of-mind. That's probably why the necklace had looked so familiar.

I grabbed the yearbook and headed back to the kitchen. On my laptop, I searched for this year's interview with Devan's parents.

"I'm outraged that nothing more is being done to find our missing daughter," Calvin Payne said, jowls jiggling and turning red with righteous outrage. "The condition of law enforcement in this state is deplorable. It's been a decade, and nothing has changed since the day our dear Devan disappeared. With all the money we've donated to the Brighton Police—"

His wife went for meek with her black A-line dress, coiffed bob, and full-carat diamond studs. But I would bet this week's donut that she truly wore the pants in the family. She shut up her husband midsentence with a side look. Her grip on his forearm had to feel like talons digging in given the size of her manicured nails and the lean strength of her privately trained muscles.

"Since no progress has been made," Felicia Payne said in a tight, sharp voice that made me wonder if she ever sang lullabies to her daughter, "we have decided to hire a new private investigator." Something they'd done every year. "Mr. Linwood Painter is renowned for his ability to locate missing children. He will arrive from Boston tomorrow. I urge" –which sounded more like *I command*— "each and every one of you to cooperate with all of his questions." The narrowing of her gaze gave a silent, *Or else*. "It is imperative we find Devan. We want our daughter home."

At least that was one sentiment I could agree with. I'd do anything to find my children were one of them missing.

The news segment flashed to the last video of Devan Payne, cheering as the Tri-Town Titans scored a touchdown against the Hopewell Hawks. Oliver Taylor, if I remember correctly.

The star of the team, who'd gone on to have a successful college career, only to have his professional career cut short on his first game with a tackle that broke his spine in two places. He was lucky to be alive. And from what I heard, he was back in the area, working as a physical therapist in Hopewell.

The camera had naturally focused on Devan's angelic face, the sun behind her gilding her in hero light. She was eating up the spotlight like it was whipped cream.

There, in the background, sat the marching band with their blue-and-gold uniforms, Cammy with her clarinet and Evie with her flute somewhere in there, getting ready for the half-time show—my favorite part of the game. To tell the truth, I didn't really understand football and found the game boring.

I'd been in the stands with my youngest, a fidgeting ten-year-old, who wanted nothing to do with sitting down and everything to do with playing with his friends. But Remy couldn't be trusted out of line of sight. He had a knack of finding trouble unless it found him first.

Harlan, too, had been there, somewhere on the grounds, keeping an eye on the crowd with then full-time officer Nolan Lander and several part-timers.

Look at that crowd, I thought. At least half the town had filled those stands to watch the area's biggest rivalry.

All those people and nobody saw anything.

One minute Devan was there cheering; the next she was gone.

My phone rang and Page's face filled my screen. "So?" she said without even a hello. "Any news?"

"I know who was in the wall."

"Who?" Page asked, breathless.

"Remember that girl who disappeared ten years ago during the homecoming football game?"

"Yeah."

"Devan Payne. Calvin and Felicia's daughter."

"They certainly wear their name well. That man wouldn't give me a small-business loan. Said I wasn't reliable enough. How is being in the same place, running a successful business for twenty-four years not reliable? I had to go to Concord to get a loan."

"Focus, Page."

She drew in a long breath. "Focusing. So, the missing Devan is the bones in the wall."

"I can't say for one hundred percent, but that necklace that was with the bones? It's the one she's wearing in the yearbook."

"I'm coming over." She rang off before I could stop her.

I started another pot of coffee and set out blondies that were going stale, then went to the door in time to catch Page's "batmobile," as she called her black-and-silver BMWi8 adorned with purple bats on the doors, screeching to a stop in the driveway.

"Keep it down," I said, inviting her in. "Harlan's sleeping."

"Sleeping? How can he be sleeping when you've solved the case?"

"It's not solved." I urged her toward the kitchen. "We just have a direction to send the medical examiner in. She can check Devan's dental records against the skull's."

Page plopped into a chair, stuffed a blondie in her mouth and washed it down with coffee. "Well? Aren't you going to wake Harlan up and tell him all this?"

"I'm going to let him sleep all he wants. He's been up for almost two days."

She harrumphed. "Fine. I'll do it."

I held her in place with a hand on her shoulder. "You will not."

"I can't just sit here and do nothing."

"Go to work."

"They won't let me in till later this afternoon." She reached for another blondie and whispered, "You know who we should talk to? Lillian Watt."

"Why?"

Page frowned. "Because it was half her wall. If it was me in her shoes, I'd want to know."

"You are a terrible gossip, Page Hamlin."

"On the contrary, I'm a great gossip. What do you say? Come with me?"

Harlan chose that moment to pad into the kitchen, still wearing yesterday's uniform. "Page, what are you doing here?"

"Apparently, your work for you."

He frowned. "It's too early for your riddles."

Harlan wiped a tired hand over his eyes and filled a mug to the top with coffee. "Who are you talking about?" he asked, as if his brain was finally catching up to the conversation.

"The girl that went missing during a football game ten years ago," Page said before I could. "Devan Payne."

He leaned his behind against the counter and drank down half the mug. "How do you know?"

I turned the yearbook to face him. There, Devan in all her blond beauty lifted her pompoms up high. The camera had caught her midjump. Flying out of the neckline of her blue-and-gold cheerleader dress, the moon and star pendant I'd glimpsed as the techs had taken photos. "That's the necklace that was in the bag last night."

That I was observant seemed to catch Harlan by surprise every single time.

"Someone could have put it there," he said. "Or dropped it when they shoved the body in the bag."

"Um," Page said, and opened her mouth to add more.

"Could be," I said, interrupting her, "but it's a place to start. The ME will have the dental records and DNA from ten years ago, so it'll be an easy comparison. It's either her or not. The ID is made or not."

He nodded, pushed off the counter and headed toward his office.

Page grabbed my arm. "Let's go."

"I shouldn't," I said, looking toward Harlan's office. He was tired. I needed to look after him.

Page tilted her head toward her shoulder and smiled. "I'll go alone."

And that would be dangerous. Page had no brakes.

OUR QUEST TO find Lillian Watt, the former owner of the Chic Boutique, in whose wall we found the bones, proved fruitless. No one answered the bell that echoed inside the cavernous interior of the brick home much too big for one little old lady. Judging from the mail overflowing her mailbox, she hadn't been there in over a week.

"Do you think she's dead?" Page asked, peeking through the faux-mullioned windows alongside the door.

"Sure, Page, let's jump right to the most outrageous conclusion."

"Well, with the mail piled high, packages under the rocker and grass halfway up my shin, what else am I supposed to think? That's just not like Lillian."

Page trotted off to the garage and peeked into the windows. "There's a car there."

"She could have gotten a ride with someone."

"It's not hers."

While trying to move Page away, I took a glance inside. A car, covered with a tarp, sat as if it hadn't seen action in a long time. Lillian drove a white Lincoln—a different shape than the tarped car.

"If her car's not there," I said, "then that's yet another reason why she's probably not murdered in her house."

I glanced around the quiet neighborhood with high-end houses. Lillian was fastidious. Every platinum hair in place, every pearl button fastened, every dab of makeup perfectly applied. She was the best poster for her shop, a lady through and through. Just in the wrong town. Brighton needed a fancy shop maybe once a year for the annual Christmas gala at the Candlewick Estate, and even then, most women made a day of shopping by going to a bigger city—Concord, Manchester, even Boston.

"We should go." I pulled on Page's purple fleece sleeve. "Before someone calls the cops."

"Good thing we know all of them."

"I'd rather not get Harlan too grumpy at me."

Page rolled her eyes with more drama than a teenager. "Fine, I want to drive by the shop and see if they've taken down the crime scene tape."

I laughed. "Can't wait to open up shop and gossip, huh?"

"Well, if you've got the goods, I always say." She batted her eyelashes.

I shook my head. "How you and Harlan are related, I have no idea."

"I have no idea either." She swung her batmobile out of the neighborhood and back toward town. She dropped me off at home, then headed to her shop.

I hadn't even walked all the way inside when Harlan glowered at me.

"What happened?"

He turned the phone so I could see the video playing on the screen. A red-faced Camden, the spitting image of her father with her dark hair and eyes, clarinet held like a bayonet, yelling at Devan Payne. "You will pay for this, Devan! I swear I'll kill you."

4

The scene stopped as if in the middle of a sentence. "Something's not right," I said, jabbing a finger at the screen of Harlan's phone. "It looks as if it's been chopped. You're only getting part of the truth. Who sent this to you?"

"Don't know."

I had a bad feeling. "When was it taken?"

"Right before Devan disappeared," he said, then took in a big breath. "Cam's going to have to come in for questioning."

"You heard back from the ME?"

He nodded. "It's Devan."

"That was fast."

"Expedited."

Of course, it was. Money bought influence. Why wasn't Harlan using his connections to help his own daughter? "You can't be serious about bringing Cammy in for questioning, Harlan! I was there. I saw her march with the band at halftime. She was in the stands for the whole game. She couldn't have killed Devan."

"It's not up to me, Ellie. I've had to recuse myself. Lander is taking over the investigation."

"Is he going to bring in Page for questioning, too? Lillian? After all, it's their wall."

"Ellie, I need you to leave this alone." He hiked his hands to his belt like I was a common criminal he had to impress with his authority. "Is that understood?"

"No, Harlan, it's not," I said, all but growling at him. He couldn't be saying he'd put his job ahead of his daughter. "This is our daughter's life we're talking about. I won't let her become a fall girl just because Calvin and Felicia Payne need someone to take the blame. You *know* she didn't do this. Don't you want to find out what really happened?"

"I do, but I can't do that if you interfere. Bringing her in is just a formality."

"Formalities can go sideways."

"I'll take her myself and make sure everything goes smoothly."

That was something anyway. "Thanks." I kissed him and hung on to his collar. "You have to promise to let me know what happens."

He gave a sharp nod and left.

Talking wasn't interfering. Camden was my daughter, and if I wanted to talk to my daughter on an ordinary Monday, I could.

I sat on the edge of the couch in the living room and called her.

"Mom, I'm busy right now." Cammy huffed as if I were a regular pest, which I wasn't. I let her have her distance. I didn't know how we'd come to have such a contentious relationship. "I can't talk."

"Your father's going to bring you in for questioning."

"What? Why?"

"We found Devan Payne's bones in Aunt Page's wall last

night. Today, someone sent him a video of you shouting at Devan that you were going to kill her."

"What? That was ten years ago! And the little you-know-what had put peanut butter on my seat, so it looked like I'd pooped myself. She made sure everybody saw and laughed at me. There was no time to change, so I had to march with that stain on my butt. She uploaded the video and everything. I was mad, but do you really believe I could kill anybody over peanut butter?"

I sighed and scanned the row of photographs along the fireplace's mantle. My three darlings growing up. "I don't, but your father is still on the way to your place and he's going to bring you in."

"This is ridiculous. I don't have time for this high school drama."

"The bones are real, Cammy. Someone killed Devan."

She paused as if finally realizing that she was in trouble. "Ooo-kay, but it wasn't me."

"I know that. I wanted to warn you and remind you not to say anything. Not even to your father. Especially not to Nolan Lander. I'm going to call Uncle Jami and have him meet you and Dad at the station."

Jamison Cruz wasn't really Cammy's uncle. He was a family friend who'd helped me and my brother pro bono after our mother died and left us homeless. My brother was seventeen then and I was about to turn fifteen. Jami got us into the Seven Angels Home for Children, which he said was a much nicer alternative to foster care. And it was, as far as those things went. The nuns were nice and took good care of us. Jami also went to bat for us, allowing my brother to emancipate and take care of me before his eighteenth birthday. Jami even gave my brother a job to help keep us afloat until we could both find our footing.

"I have a big project due by the end of the week," Cammy said. "I can't handle this right now."

I could see her now, eyes scrunched, fists at her temples as if that could calm the chaos in her mind. Cammy had always been a serious girl. She got that from her father. She tended to prefer her own company and avoid crowds. She built websites from her home office, deep in the woods between Brighton and Stoneley. She was good at it, too, having earned some awards for her designs.

"Seriously, Cam, go get this straightened out. Then you can get back to your life."

She growled. "You and Aunt Page are so dramatic!"

"Says the girl who uses too many exclamation points."

"Argh!" She hung up. I hoped I'd made my point.

In the meantime, I dialed Jami's office. I was not going to let Camden take the fall for Devan's murder. I wasn't going to let her nonchalance or Harlan's orders keep me from finding the truth to save my daughter.

"It's Ellie," I said when Jami answered. "I need you."

And even though Jami was winding down his practice and getting ready to retire, he said, "Talk to me."

PAGE WAS RIGHT. One of the first people I needed to talk to was Lillian. To my to-do list, I added a property search to find the history of the bookshop's building. I scoured social media and made a list of as many of Cam's schoolmates still living in the area as I could.

I also understood that small towns loved to rubberneck, and half the town would make an excuse to visit Page's bookshop and gawk at the hole in the wall. She would preside at the counter like a goddess. With each retelling, the story would gain detail and drama.

By the time I got to the bookshop around lunchtime, a knot of people stood around Page, listening avidly to her tale, complete with sledgehammer re-enactment. I knew all those girls from my days as a middle-school secretary.

"Are you for sure it's Devan?" Kelsey Lawrence asked, rocking from side to side, holding a newborn. She'd been in Devan's and Cam's class.

"Well, the evidence points that way," Page said with certainty. She was wearing an amethyst peasant blouse, a black broom skirt and skeleton earrings today.

"The police department got confirmation from the ME," I said.

"How did she get in there?" Morgan O'Brien asked, holding a paperback thriller. Also a classmate.

"Well, that is the question, isn't it?" Page said, leaning forward in storyteller mode. "A pretty girl like her surely had a boyfriend."

Kelsey and Morgan glanced at each other.

"She'd broken up with Oliver Taylor," Kelsey said. She raised an eyebrow. "It's always the boyfriend, right?"

Often, that was the first suspect. Back to domestics again.

"But Oliver couldn't have done it," Morgan said. "He was at the game. Scored the winning touchdown."

"According to my brother, Oliver was AWOL during the halftime pep talk. So who knows." Kelsey kissed the top of her baby's sleeping head. "There was that boy, what was his name? He had a really bad case of acne. Glasses. So skinny he looked like a breeze could blow him over."

"You mean Brent Benson?"

"Yeah." Kelsey jerked her head toward the hole in the wall over her shoulder. "That was his grandma's shop."

Morgan's face twisted with disgust. "That acne was painful to look at."

"Devan pretended he was her boyfriend for a bit," Kelsey said. "As if that was going to get Oliver to change his mind."

"Brent could barely lift his backpack, let alone a body."

Kelsey aimed her chin at Morgan's book. "You read enough of those to know that it's always who you least think is capable that's the guilty one."

A nerd spurned could turn rejection into a crime of passion.

Morgan turned the book over as if she'd find an answer in the blurb on the back cover. "True. But Brent Benson? He's still a wimp. He manages the Shaw's in Stoneley." The area's only chain supermarket. "My sister, who runs the flower department there, says the employees walk all over him."

"I've seen him there," Page said, waggling her eyebrows. "He's not skinny or ugly anymore."

"Still wimpy," Morgan insisted.

She was right. The boy had gone from Clark Kent to Superman. But apparently, his personality hadn't followed his body's transformation.

"True," Kelsey said, rocking her baby. "Devan worked at his grandma's shop for a while."

I made a note of the fact. If Devan had worked there, I definitely needed to talk to Lillian.

Morgan tapped her book once again. "He had motive. Access. And opportunity."

"Opportunity?" I asked.

"Devan paraded him in front of Oliver right before the game started. As if Brent was any threat to Oliver. I'd have gone for someone older and more handsome." Morgan, if I remembered correctly, had also cheered as part of the team.

"Yeah, but that wasn't the point," Kelsey said. "The point was to hurt Oliver, make him think that she thought Brent was better than him."

Morgan rolled her eyes. "The girl wasn't all there."

"Who else had a reason to want to hurt Devan?" I asked.

Kelsey and Morgan both made a face.

"Who didn't?" Amanda Pruitt said, joining the gossip knot. She snapped up an orange-and-green mint from the cauldron on the bestsellers' table. "She was not a happy person and that made her mean."

"To say the least," Kelsey agreed. "Nobody ever believed us when we said Devan had started whatever it was we got in trouble for." She turned to Morgan. "Remember the food fight? She got poor Jon Gilbert blamed and he got suspended for three days. That kid needed those school lunches."

He'd lived in the trailer park, the son of a single father who struggled with addiction. I remember making extra lunches and sending them home with him whenever school was out for more than a day. He'd spent a lot of time browsing Page's bookshop, and she'd given him books, pretending that it was in exchange for a review to put on a shelf talker.

"Devan set the school mascot free during the middle of a game, and Tyler Lavoie got the punishment because it was his turn to walk the dog along the sidelines."

Buster the bulldog was Principal Walker's pet and helmet-wearing mascot at home games. Students vied for the chance to show him off at games. Boys especially liked the job, because girls tended to flock around the pooch.

"She got Miss Crawford fired," Amanda said, folding the mint wrapper and tucking it in her jeans pocket.

"That's right," Kelsey said. "She slapped herself. Hard enough to leave a mark. Then she pretended Miss Crawford had done it. Just so she could get out of taking a math test."

I remember Robin's horror that a kid could have that much power over her career. She quit teaching and went on to corporate training instead.

"Then there's Anji," Morgan said with a raised eyebrow.

Anjelica Parra had been Devan's best friend in middle school. Had that changed in high school?

"Oh, wow, I'd forgotten about that," Kelsey said. Her baby started to fuss, and she stuck a pacifier in his mouth.

"What happened?" I asked.

Kelsey shook her head. "Devan somehow got hold of Anji's diary, took pics of the pages and uploaded them online for all the world to see. It was a train wreck." She blushed. "I was appalled, yet I couldn't stop reading. Super thankful it wasn't me."

Morgan nodded. "It was bad. I mean, who wants their hopes and dreams exposed. Their crushes. Anji dropped out of school and finished the year out of state. She went away to California for college."

"I heard she was back in New Hampshire," Amanda said, rolling the mint in her mouth. "Concord, I think. The AG's office. I saw her on the news not long ago."

"Who was she crushing on?" I asked.

Kelsey's baby, dressed in a tiny pumpkin suit, exercised his voice. "Gotta go. This little one needs to eat. Again. I feel like a milk cow."

She hurried out of the bookshop. Without buying anything.

"Ack, lunch is over. I need to get going, too." Morgan placed the thriller on the counter. "I'll be back for this."

And more gossip.

Amanda glanced at her Fitbit, then at the hole in the wall. "Seems kind of fitting that she ended up between two walls. She certainly squeezed enough people."

With that Amanda left, also without buying anything. People milled around the store, pretending to browse and finding a way to stop by the hole in the wall.

I turned to Page. "How are the sales today?"

She grimaced. "Not as good as I'd hoped."

"So, what's the gossip?" I asked, leaning my elbows on the checkout counter.

Page perched a hip on her high stool. "Well...everyone seems to agree that Devan was a witch, complete with broom and pointy hat. Like her father, she liked to hurt people because she could and knew she'd get away with it. Daddy could always make everything right for her."

"But he couldn't make her happy or get people to like her."

"Nope," Page said. "That gives us a long list of suspects."

"We need to narrow it down."

5

After leaving Page's bookshop, I made a stop at Town Hall to look at the history of the redbrick building where the bookshop and the boutique were housed. The building went up in 1948 and had gone through a myriad of incarnations—shoe store, newsstand, candy store— before Page had turned one half of the space into a bookshop. I couldn't find any details on renovations between incarnations. According to public records, Lillian Watt had started leasing the shop space thirteen years ago. She was the tenant when Devan was placed inside the wall. How could Lillian not have noticed fresh marks on the walls?

Unless, of course, Devan had been stuffed from Page's side of the wall. Not that Page had a mean bone in her body. She could have missed the unplanned renovations, though, because bookcases lined the wall. Except that the wall behind the bookcases had been smooth before she'd knocked a hole through it. Was it like that on Lillian's side, too? I wished I'd seen the space before Page wrecked it.

I spent way too much time looking through old editions of the *Tri-Town Times*, searching for photos and articles that featured the Pitt Building, as it was once known. I needed to talk to Lillian and ask about any renovations.

The interesting detail I uncovered was that the upper floor had once served as apartments for the shop tenants. I called Page.

"Quick question," I said, shuffling my research into a file folder and heading toward my car. "Are there any tenants in the apartments above your shop?"

"Haven't been in years. Lillian used the space as her sewing area to make alterations. Why?"

I beeped my car unlocked. "No reason, just trying to figure out if someone else might have had access to the shops when Devan went missing."

"Well—" Page started. She shuffled around and her voice went down to barely above a whisper. "When Lillian first opened, there was someone renting the apartment." Page went for the dramatic pause before she whispered, "*Robin Crawford.*"

The teacher who got fired after "slapping" Devan. I would need to talk to her. "Devan cost Robin her career. Was she mad enough to hurt the girl?"

"Anything is possible given the right circumstances." Page rang up a customer. "Hey, you're not sleuthing without me, are you?"

"No sleuthing. Just researching building history. Did you by any chance take photos of Lillian's space before you demolished the wall?"

"Of course! What are you looking for? Never mind, I'll come over after I close."

Saying no was like trying to stop a tornado. But I didn't want Harlan seeing us "interfere" with the PD's investigation. I also couldn't leave the investigation up to Lander. I didn't trust him with my daughter's future even if Harlan did. "How about if we meet at the shiny diner instead?"

Technically, the restaurant was called Pirate Pete's. Why,

nobody knew, except that Pete, the original owner had worn a scraggly beard and an eyepatch, and someone had once told him he looked like Captain Morgan of rum fame. Everybody called it the shiny diner because of the gleaming silver vintage Airstream caravan that served as the entry to the building. And on the plus side, it wasn't in Brighton but halfway to Granite Falls.

"Oh, I love their tuna melts," Page said. "Yes, let's!"

"Bring the photos."

I sat in my car, a Honda CR-V with too many miles, plotting my next move. Page closed at six on Mondays. Shaw's, I decided. That left me plenty of time to get to Pirate Pete's to meet Page. I'd go to Stoneley and see if I could talk with Brent. I needed to pick up eggs and English muffins anyway, so technically I wasn't snooping, but grocery shopping. If I happened to run into Brent, well, what was I supposed to do, be rude and not speak to him?

Once there, I headed to the customer service booth, garish with its over-the-top Halloween ghosts, goblins and broom-riding witches, and asked to speak with Brent, who definitely had changed since high school. He'd gone from skinny to buff. I could almost see a six-pack under his white shirt and green tie. Gone, too, was the acne. Even the scars had somehow smoothed out. His blond hair sported a stylish cut. And he wore contacts instead of glasses.

I met him by the aisle overflowing with bagged candy and decorated with hay bales and plastic jack-o'-lanterns. My ruse was asking for dark-chocolate-covered digestive cookies. Even though the store had a British section, they rarely carried the chocolate-covered digestives.

"I'll see what I can do," Brent said and half turned to leave.

"Hey, by the way, I stopped by to talk to your grandmother yesterday and she wasn't home. Is everything okay?"

"She went to visit her sister in Florida."

Without stopping the mail? "Do you know when she'll be back?"

He shrugged. "Today, I think. Or tomorrow. It depends on when the cheaper flight was." He narrowed his gaze at me. "What do you need with her?"

I didn't exactly run in Lillian's social circle, so my seeking her out was out of the ordinary.

"Just a quick question." I waved at him as if to go on with my shopping, then turned back. "Did you hear about your grandmother's shop?"

The hangry dinner crowd jostled around us, aiming carts toward the speediest cashier.

"It's been closed for a while," he said, gaze roving over the crowd. "It's nothing new."

"I mean the body that was found in the wall."

He flinched as if I'd hit him. "The what?"

"Body. Devan Payne."

His tanned face blanched. "Hadn't heard anything about that."

"There's a rumor she was dating you senior year."

He made a sour-lemon face. "Yeah, you know how accurate rumors are. Not very. She pretended she liked me when Oliver Taylor was around, then treated me like a leper the rest of the time. I have no idea what game she was playing."

"That must have hurt."

"That was just Devan," he said like it was no big thing, but the sting of it still tainted his voice.

The angel's face with the devil's heart. "Were you at the football game that day?"

"I never went to football games. I was at my friend Jason's, playing video games. Like we always did. Nerds unite, you know." His eye twitched and his fingers curled. He was lying. Morgan had seen him there.

"You think Oliver could've killed Devan?"

Brent huffed out a rough laugh. "Oliver was done with her after what she did to Anji." The loudspeaker crackled, calling him back to work. He pointed at the amorphous voice. "I gotta go."

What she'd done to Anji seemed the thing that put Devan's behavior over the top for a lot of her classmates. If she could wreck her best friend's life, she could hurt anybody. And nobody wanted to end up her victim. "Okay, well, thanks for looking into those cookies for me."

"No problem."

But his stiff gait as he strode away toward his office suggested that my questions had indeed caused him a problem. Why was he lying about being at the game?

Jason Parra, I thought. Anji's twin brother. Two birds; one stone.

UNFORTUNATELY FOR ME, Jason Parra no longer lived in the area. He worked as a game designer in California, according to his LinkedIn page. His company was poised to put out the biggest game of their history. He didn't answer his phone. I sent him an email but wasn't holding my breath for an answer.

Anji was similarly unavailable. I also left her a message and sent an email. Somehow, I doubted she'd want to revisit the most painful part of her childhood. But I had to find a way to talk to her.

In the meantime, I made a call, then a slight detour to the Hopewell Medical Center next to the hospital. I was halfway there anyway. I would casually arrange to run into Oliver Taylor as he finished his shift at the physical therapy center.

Oliver Taylor was the kind of handsome boy that made girls go gaga over him, doodling their names and his in hearts all over their notebooks. Teen idol pretty. And though he walked

with a certain stiffness now, he was still handsome enough to
make girls dream. I'd bet he was a popular therapist.

Phone in hand, I zipped toward the door and bumped into
him on purpose. "Oh, I'm so sorry. Here I am texting and walking, what I always tell my kids not to do."

He smiled, a smile gorgeous enough to make even a middle-
aged woman want to sigh. "No harm done."

"Oh, my. You're Oliver Taylor, aren't you? The football star
from Brighton and UNH."

He gave a crooked smile. "A long time ago."

I leaned toward him conspiratorially. "Did you hear about
your girlfriend?"

"Which one?" He chuckled as if he had a long train of
women vying for his attention. He probably did.

"Devan Payne."

The friendliness melted from his face. "She hasn't been
around for a long time."

"They found her. Yesterday. In the wall between The Purple
Page and the Chic Boutique."

"What?" He looked at me as if I'd sprouted horns.

"You were her boyfriend."

He shook his head. "Nah, we were over long before she
disappeared." He hooked a thumb toward the parking lot. "Hey,
listen, I've got to go."

"Where did you go during halftime?" I asked, following him
to the silver Jeep with the blue trim.

His brows scrunched down. "Who are you? The police?"

A mom worried about her kid taking the rap for someone
else's bad deed. "Just curious."

He jerked the Jeep's door open. "You know what they say
about curiosity."

I dipped my head to one side in question.

He tried to smile, but it looked more like a sneer. "It killed
the cat."

THE NEXT MORNING, before the sun was even up, Harlan padded into the kitchen and headed straight to the coffeepot. I hadn't heard him coming, so the evidence of my "interference" was still splayed across the whole tabletop. As he filled his mug, back to me, I tried to surreptitiously gather all the papers and turn the page of the pad to a fresh sheet where I scribbled Grocery List across the top.

"I thought you had the day off today," I said, noting he was dressed in his uniform again.

He turned and leaned against the counter, sipping his coffee. "There's a lot going on right now, Ellie. Nolan needs Micah's help."

"So, you're taking patrol." Of course, he was. "What happened to winding down, going part-time so you could retire in the spring?"

"That's where the rookie comes in."

I got up and headed to the fridge to make him breakfast.

"Law enforcement isn't exactly a coveted career these days," Harlan said. "Especially in these backwoods. We really need about double the officers we have."

In other words, if he retired before he died, I'd be lucky. "What's happening with Camden?"

"She was cleared."

I slammed the fridge door closed and spun to face Harlan. "You could have led with that! Why didn't you tell me last night?"

"You were asleep when I came in."

Given my insomnia troubles, I supposed I should be thankful he'd let me sleep.

"That boy she was seeing in high school, Alex Powers, had shot a video that day for his college application to film school. Lucky for us, he had stars in his eyes when it came to Camden and made her practically the star of the show. She was there the whole time. He even had her and Evie coming out of the band room to meet you and Remy."

My whole body sagged with relief. "Thank God for that."

"Camden's cleared," he said again, then dropped his gaze to the file folder and pad of paper. "You've got to let this go, Ellie."

"Of course." I stuffed the pad of paper inside the file and closed the cover. "That's all I wanted—to clear Camden." But the unanswered questions roiled like a stormy sea. The need for answers made my fingers twitch. I hunted for a small skillet in the cabinet by the stove and turned on a burner.

"You might have cost us our prime suspect." His features turned stony, and his eyes burned with the anger he fought to contain.

"What?" I cracked an egg in a bowl and scrambled it with a fork. "Who?"

He lifted his phone from his pocket, stabbed at the screen a couple of times, then showed me a photo. Me confronting Oliver at the medical center. The photo looked grainy, as if it had come from a security camera.

The egg sizzled when it hit the pan. "I was there to get some paperwork for the bloodwork I need to get before my physical next week."

Which reminded me that I really needed to pick it up and stop by the lab.

"Whatever you said spooked him." Harlan stuffed his phone back in his pocket. "He wasn't home and didn't show up for work this morning."

Suspicious behavior. But still, it felt wrong. "If it makes you feel better, I don't think Oliver killed Devan."

"It doesn't. Why do you think he's innocent?"

Gut wasn't acceptable in a court of law, but I found mine was more often right than wrong. "He didn't have time in the twenty minutes of halftime to find, kill and hide Devan, even if he had stashed her in an interim spot."

"So where was he?"

"That, I don't know." Yet.

I realized I'd forgotten to toast the English muffin and placed both halves in the toaster oven. Then went to the fridge for a slice of Cheddar. Where had Oliver gone and why?

"Plus, Devan was in the past for him." I watched the cheese melt over the egg. "He dumped her after what she did to Anji Parra. And his mind was on Anji."

The toaster oven dinged.

"Here's something that you're not privy to as a civilian." His voice was unnervingly gentle and yet laced with thunder. "The duffel with the bones belonged to Oliver Taylor."

6

"Tell Lander to look at Brent Benson," I told Harlan as I handed him a plate with his breakfast sandwich. "He's lying about being at the game. The bones were in his grandmother's shop. And he had more than one reason to want to hurt Devan. And don't say he wasn't strong enough to do it. Anger, as you know, gives the weak wings."

He wrapped the sandwich in a napkin, twined an arm around my shoulders and kissed me. "Leave it alone, Ellie. If you don't mind your own business, someone's going to get hurt. And I don't want it to be you."

After Harlan left, I sagged onto a kitchen chair, staring at my file folder. Had I really caused Oliver to run? Was my gut wrong this time?

Curiosity kills, Oliver had implied. And the shiver that had gone down my spine at that moment made me glad we were in a public space with witnesses. Although he had the muscle and the motive to murder Devan, I didn't really think he'd had the opportunity, nor the desire. He was more worried about Anji's state of mind than revenge against Devan.

But how had the bones ended up in his duffel bag?

I RAN into Lillian Watt at the post office. I'd come to mail a care package to Remy, who was a senior at Emerson College where he studied Sports Communications, of all things. His favorite— S'more cookies. When I got stressed, I baked, so my kitchen counter now held three kinds of cookies, cooling on racks.

Lillian wore a long-sleeved black dress that flared at the hips, topped with a light beige cashmere coat with a chic rhinestone pin in the shape of a fall sunflower. She was arguing with the postmaster through the half door where a garland of bats and pumpkins dangled.

"I have the proof," she said in a stern, schoolmarmish way, platinum chignon shaking. She switched her silver-headed ebony cane from one hand to the other, then plucked a sheet of paper from her black patent-leather handbag. "I stopped mail delivery for eleven days. I *specifically* said I would stop by and pick it up. Do you know what I found when I got back, young man? A glaring advertisement that no one was home. Mail overflowed the box and packages littered the porch. That's an invitation for burglars. It's irresponsible behavior."

"I'm sorry, ma'am," the postmaster said with an air of resignation. He probably wished he was wearing a tactical vest to divert her verbal bullets. "We never got the order."

"The price of postage keeps going up and the service quality down." Lillian huffed, brandishing her cane. She stuffed the paper back in her purse. "How is that any way to run a business?"

Cane hitting the wooden floor hard enough to leave a divot, she swiveled to leave.

I intercepted her. "Are you all right?"

She shook her head in short strokes. "I come back from vacation only to have to deal with complete incompetence."

"Can I buy you a cup of tea?"

She finally looked up at me, scrunching her gaze, showing off the deep creases at her corners of eyes and mouth. "Why?"

"You look like you could use one."

She sighed long and deep. "I could, actually. That's very kind of you."

We strolled in silence to the Brightside Bakery. Lillian leaned heavily on her cane, so the pace was slow. The cold wind whipped right through my too-thin cardigan. The gray skies above promised rain before the day's end. Lillian ordered an Earl Grey tea and a pumpkin scone, and I got a cup of coffee and a pumpkin spice muffin.

"How was your visit with your sister?" I asked after Lillian seemed to relax a bit.

"How did you know?"

"I ran into Brent at Shaw's yesterday, and he mentioned it."

She added a drop of milk and a spoonful of sugar to her tea. "He's a good boy, Brent. He's always looking after me."

"It's nice that he's around."

She nodded. "My sister fell and broke her arm. I went to help her out for a few days."

"That's so kind of you."

Lillian gave a small nod. "Well, she helped me when I broke my hip. We're at that age, you know. Her daughter wants to put her in one of those old people homes, but Lydia would rather stay in her own home. I can't blame her."

"Me either."

She popped a morsel of scone in her mouth. "I'm thinking of moving there so we can help each other out."

"That sounds like a good solution." I pointed at the cane. "Is that why you need a cane, because of your hip injury?"

"It never did set properly." She broke off another piece of scone. "That's why I opened my boutique, you know."

"Because of your hip?"

"I couldn't find anything fashionable that would be loose

enough around the hips." She tsked. "As if anyone would want to wear a shapeless muumuu just because of a bad hip."

"Your shop did have beautiful outfits. I bought several dresses for the Christmas gala over the years."

"Yes, well, right shop. Wrong town. My Albert loved it here. We'd raised our family here. So, when he passed, I stayed. The boutique helped keep me busy."

"I was sorry to see you close after Labor Day."

"It was getting to be too much for me to run, especially now that it's so hard to get any help." She waved in the vicinity of her face. "My eyes aren't what they used to be, so I couldn't do the alterations anymore."

"You're not the only one who's had to close."

"No." She glanced wistfully out the window at Main Street where several other storefronts stood dark and empty.

"You heard about what happened at The Purple Page?" I said, smoothing out any accusation in my voice.

She shook her head and sipped her tea.

"They found a body in the wall."

Her mouth twisted with disgust. "How is that even possible?"

"Did you do any renovations while you owned the shop?"

She shook her head. "Nothing big. I had the walls repainted several times over the years. I changed the layout once or twice a year. But nothing that would involve making a hole in the wall." She carefully set her cup back in her saucer. "Do they know whose body it was?"

"The rumor is it was Devan Payne, the girl that disappeared ten years ago. Didn't she work for you?"

She made an exaggerated shiver. "I did make the mistake of hiring that girl as a favor to her mother. She had no sense of decorum and insulted my customers. I had to fire her."

The bakery's door opened with the *boo, whoo, whoo* of a mechanical ghost, shivering by the big picture window. The baby in the stroller startled and cried. The mom gently laughed as she comforted her daughter.

"I hear Devan was dating Brent during the time she disappeared," I said and popped the last of the muffin in my mouth. The buttery pecan crumb topping made me want to trot back to the counter to buy another one.

Lillian's pale blue eyes went hard as marbles. "Brent had nothing to do with that girl's disappearance. He wasn't even at the game. He always played video games with his friend Jason." She pushed the scone plate away. "Besides, that girl weighed more than Brent did back then. He couldn't have stuffed her in the wall even if he'd wanted to. And, as I said, no holes were made."

"It's a mystery, all right." Sensing she was done talking about Devan, I brought the conversation back to Florida, then excused myself. "It was so nice to chat with you, Lillian. Did you want me to have Harlan send extra patrols by your house?"

"Whatever for?"

"In case someone didn't get the memo you were back home."

She batted away my concern. "I have an alarm system and I keep it armed."

I STOPPED by the bookshop to fill Page in on my encounter with Lillian. Construction was in full swing, filling the shop with the sounds of saws and hammers and the scents of drywall dust and sawdust.

"Could Lillian have stuffed Devan in the wall?" I wondered.

Page wrapped order sheets around books customers had requested and shelved them behind her. "She fired her, so she had no reason to kill the girl. Plus, she was always asking people to lift things for her. I carried boxes for her all the time. She couldn't have done it by herself."

"With Brent's help?"

"Maybe."

"Want to come to a yoga class with me?" I asked Page.

She exaggerated a shudder. "No, thanks, but let me know how it goes."

Being a small-town mom, the chief of police's wife, working at the school while the kids were growing up, helping Page at the bookshop when she needed help, all made it so that I knew just about everyone in town. I knew their relationships. I knew many of their habits. And Angela Parra, Anji's mom, worked as a dental assistant and took a yoga class at lunchtime. She had the lithe body to prove it.

I stuffed myself into black yoga pants and a loose hay-colored tunic adorned with pumpkins and headed to the Blue Lotus Yoga Studio. Rain poured down in a deluge, making driving difficult. But I wasn't going to let a little downpour stop me. I paid for a one-class pass, and spotted Angela right away. I silently groaned. Of course, she would choose a spot right up front.

I chitchatted with her for a few minutes while we waited for class to start. Then as the minute hand ticked closer to the hour, I broached the real reason for attempting to contort my unwilling body into a pretzel. "I saw Anji on TV the other day. She looked so smart and professional. You must be so proud of her."

Angela's smile made her eyes twinkle. "I am. She's going places, my Anji."

"Is she living in Concord?"

Angela stretched out her legs and curled her torso forward, her forehead almost touching her knees. "Manchester. She's got a small penthouse apartment with a great view, right in the heart of downtown."

"I'm surprised she would come back to New Hampshire."

"Why?" Angela stretched her arms up and sideways.

I lifted an eyebrow. "What happened in high school."

She switched sides. "Like you said, that was high school."

"You've heard about Devan?"

"All I can say is that girl got what she deserved." She twisted, one hand on her knee, the other behind her. "I know, not very Zen, but she was a mean...witch."

"Have the police talked to Anji?"

The twist unwound with the speed of a striking snake. "Are you implying Anji is responsible for Devan's death?"

"Of course not!"

Angela cranked her chin up. "She's a lawyer. She was vetted forward and backward before being offered the job at the AG's office. If there was anything to find, someone would have found it back then. Plus, Anji was at her grandparents' in Boston when Devan disappeared. She needed a break after—well, after what Devan did to her." Angela's eyes brimmed with tears. "We almost lost her, you know. Jason found her. I shudder to think what would have happened if he hadn't. I don't even know where she got the pills."

"I didn't know. I'm so sorry. Camden was one of her victims, too."

Angela stabbed a finger at the floor between us. "You know what I felt when the news came Devan had disappeared? I felt a sigh of relief. She wasn't going to hurt my baby ever again."

Soft music tinkled through the speakers and Zoe Carpenter took her place at the head of the class. "Let's start with some breathing. Inhale for three and exhale for six. Let your attention sink from your head to your heart. Forget your problems for right now."

Easier said than done.

Would Jason have wanted to avenge his sister?

WHEN I GOT HOME after the yoga class ended at one, Lander waited, sitting on the front stoop, letting the rain wash over him. His arms hung off his knees. His spine curled as if he carried a heavy burden. I almost felt sorry for him. But the inclination disappeared as soon as he unwound and stood, gaze narrow, mouth hard.

"Where have you been?" he asked, his tone both hard and brittle, rainwater dripping from his hair onto his face like tears. "Don't you ever answer your phone?"

I edged past him to unlock the door. "None of your business. But if you must know, I was at a yoga class, and they require you to turn off your phone."

He grabbed my forearm to keep me from going inside. "Elize..."

He never called me by my full name. So I looked up.

That's when I noticed the pain twisting his features. My whole body went icy with alarm. "No, don't say it." I tried to pull away from his grip. He hung on. My heart raced, shattered. "Don't you dare say it!"

"Not Harlan," he said.

I sighed with relief. "Who?"

"Owen."

"Oh, no. Poor Evie!" I had to get to her before she heard the news from the gossip tree.

I yanked the door open to go get changed.

"Elize..."

I turned my head, dread mounting fast and hard.

"Harlan's hurt."

7

Three days later, on a glorious fall afternoon, sparkling with sunshine and a riot of colors, I stood by my daughter's boyfriend's grave. Friday the thirteenth. The unluckiest of days. Owen's parents had wanted a quick funeral. But him being a cop, even if a new one, and having died on duty meant that this couldn't be a private family moment. A whole cordon of law enforcement officers from all over the state still showed up to honor him.

One by one, they shook Owen's parents' hands, said their condolences, but their sad eyes all said, *Thank God it wasn't me.*

Sobs echoed through the gathered crowd. So many people. Owen had grown up here and most of the town had also shown up to support his parents and older brother.

An accident, Lander had said. Harlan and Owen had responded to a call about a stranded motorist. They'd helped a young girl with a flat tire. Harlan had sat her in the cruiser to keep her out of the rain while Owen set out to put on her spare because the area's one tow truck was busy elsewhere.

A rubbernecker hit both while they worked on the side of the road, then sped away. The driver had probably hydroplaned with all the rain, Lander said. And just left them there, bleeding and broken on the side of the road.

Owen. Dead. Gone.

Harlan with a concussion and broken leg that had required surgery to insert pins.

It didn't make sense. Owen was so young. Just starting his career. Doing a good deed.

Harlan stood on crutches, head bandaged, with the rest of the department, guilt etched all over his face. He should still be at home, resting. He could be the one lying in that grave. I felt guilty that I was thankful he wasn't.

Harlan was determined to find the hit-and-run driver. But there were no cameras in that part of town. No witnesses to the hit-and-run, except the panicked teen driver. And she couldn't say anything more than it was a big, black, old-fashioned car. That it had hit the officers, crushed them against the teen's car, backed up, and raced off as if the devil were on its tail.

And because Harlan had hit his head hard on the pavement, he couldn't remember the accident.

How could anyone be so callous? To just leave two men like that, dying, without helping them.

My thoughts were a swarm of gnats that couldn't settle. I held on to Evie, who soaked my shoulder with her tears. She was my sensitive child, the one who felt every nuance of a conversation at skin level. The one who couldn't bear tags in her clothes because they itched too much. Her relationship with Owen was still new but that didn't mean the loss didn't hurt.

The flag-draped coffin brought back memories of putting my brother to rest all those years ago. The way it had gutted me. If I hadn't gotten pregnant with Remy soon after, I wasn't sure I would have survived.

Poor Evie, I felt for her, having her heart broken so young. I was glad she had a job she loved that she could lose herself into. Having to put on a smile for her class of kindergartners would help her get through the grief. And she had a whole support system at home and at work. She'd get through this.

I didn't hear a word of the remembrances, of the readings, of the eulogies, concentrating instead on Evie.

Someone handed Owen's mother the folded flag. She pressed it into her husband's hands as if it were made of poison.

Evie pulled out of my arms and rushed to the nearest tree to retch, even though her stomach was empty.

I started toward her, but Cammy stopped me. "Let her be for a minute."

I gave Cam a hug. "You're right. Why don't you get Aunt Page to the community center for the gathering."

Cam, ever practical, asked, "How will you get there if I take your car?"

"We'll get Lander to drive the three of us."

I leaned my back against the wide trunk of the ancient maple tree, flaming in shades of yellows, oranges and reds, blind to the soothing resting place the cemetery's caretakers had created.

Voices, like the buzz of mosquitoes, carried on the breeze.

"My guy says the tracks are deliberate," a voice I didn't recognize said. "It has nothing to do with my investigation into Devan Payne's disappearance, but I thought you might want to know."

The PI the Paynes had hired?

"Are you sure?" Lander asked, voice sharp as a fillet knife.

"One hundred percent."

Every cell in my body twanged. Deliberate? Someone had wanted to murder Owen and Harlan?

I rammed my way to where Lander and another, leaner man stood by the gaping hole of Owen's grave. Both turned and looked at me like moose watching an out-of-control semi barreling their way.

"What do you mean, deliberate?" This was my fault. Harlan was right. If I hadn't listened to my stupid brain's impulse, if I'd stopped asking questions, if I hadn't kept going after Camden was cleared, then Owen would still be alive, and Harlan wouldn't be hurt.

He signaled the other man, who nodded and left. "Ellie—"

"Was Harlan the one meant to die?" *It should've been you*, I thought and didn't care how unkind it was. *You should've been on patrol, not Harlan.*

"You really need to stay out of this," Lander said, trying to turn me toward the row of cars along the side of the path. "The whole department is working on this."

"What? All two of you?" Then I waved my comment away. This wasn't his fault. "Brent Benson," I said, voice thick. "You have to look at Brent Benson. He wasn't happy with my questions. And he's got a lot to lose if he goes to prison."

"He was at the urgent care, getting stitched up after an accident at work."

"How convenient." I scrunched my eyes closed tight, trying to slow the manic ping-pong of my thoughts.

"You're speculating and that—"

"Has no place in an investigation." According to Harlan, anyway. But you had to look at the what-ifs to come up with a direction.

"*Something* had to tip you off—or that Boston PI Felicia Payne hired," I said. "It was raining. It could've been an accident."

Please, let it be just an accident. I couldn't live with myself if I'd caused Owen's death.

"The driver made no attempt to stop," Lander said, his eyes an emotionless bronze wall. "Harlan told me to tell you he loved you in case..."

He didn't make it. My throat spasmed. The guilt, so intense, all but ripped me apart.

I love you, too, Harlan. So much.

I would give up all our plans. I would watch him work every day of his life, if we could just grow old together. We'd made a good life together. I wanted it to last.

"Can you give Evie and me a ride to the community center? Cammy took Page with my car."

He gave one sharp nod.

After we got home, I settled an exhausted Harlan into bed, Stella at his feet. I curled at the edge of the bed to give him room, my mind filling with all the could-haves. This could have been Harlan's funeral. I could be in bed alone right now. I had to start being thankful for what I already had, to be happy with what was instead of resentful because our retirement plan was taking longer than expected to come about.

But as I stared at the ceiling that night, listening to Harlan's unconscious moans of pain, I knew that if I was the cause of Harlan's pain, I had to do everything in my power to bring the hit-and-run driver to justice.

I tossed away the sheet and blanket and got up.

I had to go back to square one.

I'd missed something.

FOCUSING on going over my notes, flushing them out, kept the night from lasting an eternity. That, and baking. By the time the sun came up, I had apple cider muffins and apple oatmeal scones and a pumpkin coffee cake taking up most of the counter space.

The contents of my research file were lined up on the kitchen table, and I tried to reorder the notes until they made sense. But even a pot of coffee wasn't helping. Why would anyone want to hurt Harlan and Owen? Especially in Brighton where Harlan was such a big part of the community and Owen a long-time resident.

Page arrived just after seven, still dressed in her bright-orange bat-and-ghost-decorated pajama bottoms, purple Trick-or-Treat T-shirt, purple fleece robe and pumpkin felt slippers.

"I couldn't sleep," she said and dove right into the coffee cake, cutting a slice big enough to feed the whole family. "Evie still here?"

"She's in her old room. Cammy insisted on going home. Remy went to Jami's." Who was like a grandfather to him. "He'll drive Remy back to Boston tomorrow."

She looked up with red-rimmed eyes. "I can't believe we almost lost Harlan."

"But we didn't, and that's what we have to focus on."

Page nodded, then spied my notes. "Where are we?"

Instead of dealing with the what-ifs, I planned on throwing myself full tilt into the investigation. I went to pour myself a cup of coffee and found the carafe empty, so I started another pot.

"I missed something," I said. "Something important. Something that made someone afraid enough they felt they had to run Harlan over."

"No, Ellie." Her eyes brimmed with tears. Harlan was the last of her family of origin. Both their parents had died long ago. And Harlan watched out for Page in a myriad of ways. Even though she gave him a hard time, she loved him. "It was an accident."

"Lander and that detective from Boston don't think so." What if it wasn't me, I thought, who'd scared someone? What if it was that detective asking more pointed questions than I did? "I need to find out who Linwood Painter talked to."

Page pushed away the cake she'd been shoveling in her mouth as if she could block the pain of her brother's near loss by filling herself up with carbs. "I'm going with you."

"What about the shop?"

"You were right," she said, heading toward my bedroom. I followed her, hoping she wouldn't wake up Harlan. "It's better if there's no one there while the renovations are going on."

I didn't want to deal with Page's tears, which were apt to flow like Niagara Falls. But I got where she was coming from. Doing something was better than moping around, letting guilt engulf you. She rifled through my closet and plucked out a pair of beige hiking pants and a magenta fleece jacket. I urged her back out of the room.

"Lander said that Brent Benson was in the hospital when —" I swallowed hard. "I think we should go talk to him. I just can't shake the feeling that he had something to do with Devan's disappearance."

"I heard he had a concussion when he fell off a ladder." Page changed into the hiking pants, then zipped the fleece over her T-shirt. "He's staying at Lillian's, so you have the perfect excuse to drop by."

I raised my eyebrows at her.

"The muffins. We'll bring him some muffins as an excuse to check on him."

8

W aiting for an acceptable hour to stop by Lillian's on a Saturday morning seemed to drag on forever. Page helped me make giveaway packages of pastry in containers I'd recycled. Enough gift boxes to make anyone we chose to interview feel guilty and talk to us.

"Can't we go now?" Page asked, pacing the kitchen like a caged hamster between filling Stella Luna's food bowl and refilling her water bubbler.

"Too early. But—" I sat at the kitchen table, turned over to a fresh sheet on the pad of paper and, looking at my notes lined up on the table, dialed the number for Jason Parra. When he answered, I hit Record.

"Do you know what time it is?" he asked in a sleepy voice.

I did. That's why I'd called, hoping to catch him before he got up. "This is Elize Hamlin from Brighton. I'd like to ask you a few questions about what you remember from the night Devan Payne disappeared."

"Devan Payne! I haven't heard that name in years."

Page scooched her chair closer to hear and nearly knocked

the phone out of my hand. I set it on the table and hit Speaker. "They found her in the wall in a shop downtown."

"Whoa! That's sick!"

"Were you at the game that day?"

Page reached for the lone apple cider muffin left on the counter and settled in as if this were one of the podcasts she listened to all day at work.

"Nah, Brent and I couldn't stand football. We played video games at my house."

"Except that Brent was caught on tape, being paraded by Devan along the sidelines."

A rustle of bedsheets filled the air. "Look, the girl was a user. She used Brent to try to hurt Oliver. When that didn't work, she dumped him like he was garbage."

"That gives him motive."

The pad of feet, first on carpet, then on tile. "Uh, did you see what we looked like back then?"

Brent, skinny and pimply. Jason, tubby with Coke-bottle glasses.

"Two nerds equal one jock?" I said.

He chuckled. From the background came the distinctive sounds of a Keurig brewing. "Yeah, if only."

"Someone killed her, Jason. And you and Brent had a lot of reasons to want to get back at her. Like you said, she was a manipulator."

"What's it to you anyway? I remember you from middle school. You a cop now?"

Just as he'd twisted the truth to spare himself, I edited it now for my purposes. "My daughter Camden was brought in for questioning. She didn't do it. I need to make sure she doesn't take the fall for someone else."

"Yeah, Devan got Cammy good." He gave a long sigh. "Look, we did go to the high school that day. We were going to disable Devan's car, so that she'd get stranded."

"You cut her brakes?" Page asked, eyes going wide. She had a knack for going straight to the direst possibility.

"Uh, no. Why would you even say that? We were going to loosen the battery but couldn't figure out how to get in the car." He sounded embarrassed at the fact. "Cell phone reception in the back of the lot isn't the best."

Meaning, they couldn't look up how to disable the car. Kids with cars had to park at the back of the lot, where there was no camera coverage, so that paying spectators could park closer to the field. "So, what, you just left?"

"We, uh, keyed her brand-new car. And ran back to my place." Jason snorted. "Brent had to use his inhaler. I thought I was going to pass out. Talk about nerd clichés."

His account sounded so plausible, I wanted to believe him.

"Look, she almost caused my sister's death," Jason said. "I was mad, and I wanted her to hurt, but I wouldn't have killed her. And back then, she was a lot stronger than either me or Brent. That's why we went for her car."

Page scribbled Oliver across a napkin and held it up, waving it to catch my attention.

"What about Oliver?" I asked, pushing the napkin away from my face. "Do you think he could have killed Devan?"

"If it wasn't for the fact that half the town had eyes on him for the whole game, I'd say maybe." A fridge opened, buzzed, then closed with a sucking sound.

How could Oliver have killed her with so many witnesses watching him every second of the game, except for at halftime when he disappeared? "He was seeing Anji."

Jason slurped coffee. "After Devan put Anji's diary out there? Telling the world about her crush on Oliver? She didn't want anything to do with him. She was too embarrassed. I mean, those thoughts were supposed to be private, so she wrote some pretty cheesy things, you know." He paused as if he was reliving the chaos of those days. "She couldn't go back to school. The thought of everyone laughing at her, knowing how she felt, especially Oliver, made her take a bunch of sleeping pills."

"I'm so sorry that happened."

"Thing is, Oliver did like her. That's one of the reasons he dumped Devan. Anji was sweet—still is. A nice girl who went out of her way to help people. And Devan...well, Devan, she couldn't stand that Oliver liked Anji better than her."

"Were you at the school at halftime?" I asked, hoping he'd seen something that could help.

"No, we were huffing and puffing in my basement. Scared Officer Hamlin was going to come knocking at the door to arrest us for vandalism."

The mention of Harlan's name made my heart squeeze at what I almost lost. I closed my eyes and swallowed hard. *Keep it together, Ellie.*

The worst part was that I believed Jason. So, if he and Brent hadn't killed Devan, who had?

AFTER CHECKING on Harlan and Evie, Page and I headed out.

Our visit to Lillian's was a bust. She wouldn't let us in, insisting Brent needed to rest after his ordeal. She did, however, accept the container of pastry.

"We should have put a listening device in the box," Page said, fiddling with the edge of the fleece jacket. "I'd give anything to be a fly on the wall."

She rifled through the console for the bag of mints I kept there. "What now?"

"I don't think Brent did it." I sighed, tapping my fingertips against the steering wheel. "I don't think Oliver did it either. And those were our two most likely suspects."

She rolled the mint around her mouth. "What did Oliver do during those twenty minutes at halftime?"

"That is the question. He did warn me that curiosity killed. And nobody can find him now." Made me wish I'd put a tracking device on him. I waved the thought away. Hanging out with Page so much was clouding my judgment.

"What about Robin Crawford?" Page tapped the suspect list page propped on her knees. "She lives in Stoneley now and does corporate trainings, mostly online." Page gave me an exaggerated smile, showing way too much teeth, and plucked at the hiking pants. "She's part of the Second Saturday Hiking Club."

"How do you know that?"

Page raised a shoulder. "She mentioned it when she bought a book on hiking in New Hampshire."

"You want to go hiking?" I said, doubtful. Page didn't believe in exercise of any kind.

Her face turned serious. "I want Owen's killer to die of old age in prison. If that means hiking, so be it."

That was how we ended up at the Stoneley Town Forest, a dozen costumed hikers—from Big Foot to witches to skeletons—milling around us, ready to hike to the top of Mt. Candle.

I glanced at Page's bright-orange pumpkin slippers and sighed. I kept a pair of hiking boots in the trunk—you never knew when they would come in handy. I changed into the boots and handed Page my sneakers.

"Oh, I suppose those would work better," she said, sitting on the bumper and throwing her slippers over her shoulder into the trunk.

"You didn't get the memo?" the clipboard-laden hike organizer said, looking down her long nose at our outfits. "Where are your costumes?"

"I'm Dora, the Explorer," Page said, without missing a beat, hiking the purple backpack she used as a purse over her shoulders.

"I'm a newbie hiker," I said, which sounded ridiculous, but I wasn't as fast as Page when it came to comebacks.

The too-skinny organizer huffed and headed toward the trail head. "All right, people. Do *not* stray from the trail. Do *not* litter. Pick a buddy and stick with them. Stay on the trail and you can't get lost. There's a two-thousand-foot elevation change. If you can't keep up"–she stared pointedly at Page— "head back to the parking lot."

She unfolded a map and traced the trail. "Today's route is the Rainbow Waterfall Loop. It will take us up, over and around the mountain."

Page leaned close and jabbed at my arm with a finger. "She's here," she whispered, aiming her chin at a woman holding a leashed German Shepard, standing at the edge of the gathered crowd. "Robin Crawford."

Robin had chosen a ghost bride costume, complete with a long gray wig with black veil, gray raggy dress, black tights with gray ribbon accents, and a bouquet of black roses tucked into her belt. She'd whitened her face and darkened circles around her eyes so that they looked hollow. The Shepard wore a black cape with bat wings at his shoulders.

Even with the costume, she didn't look as if she'd aged well since she'd left Brighton. The pancake makeup accented the permanent frown creasing her forehead and the marionette lines slashing the sides of her mouth.

"She's got to use the beauty filter when she does those Zoom classes," Page said with a cluck. I shushed her with an elbow to the ribs.

The hike was no walk in the park, and even though I walked a lot with Stella Luna, my lungs and thighs soon burned on the climb. Good thing for us, Robin kept to the back of the pack, holding her dog on a short leash.

"Is he friendly?" Page asked, stretching a hand toward the dog.

"Not particularly."

At the dog's warning growl, Page snapped her hand back.

"Oh, my goodness! I remember you," Page said, pretending she'd just recognized Robin. "You used to live above the bookstore."

Robin narrowed her gaze at Page. "Ah, the bookstore lady."

"You heard what happened, right?"

Robin cranked up an eyebrow.

"Devan Payne." Page leaned closer, but hopped back when the dog, bat wings waggling, growled at her again. "She was found in the wall between my shop and Lillian's. Lillian was your landlord, wasn't she?"

"Are you implying that I had something to do with *that*?" Robin's already white skin paled to ghost.

"Of course not," I said, trying to defuse the situation. "We were just wondering if you heard anything that day."

"I wasn't living there anymore when Devan disappeared." Robin sped up, raggy ribbons streaming after her, trying to lose us.

"That's right, you broke your lease," Page said, trotting back to Robin. Page's voice was breathy. Sweat beaded at her hairline. "I remember Lillian being upset about that."

"Well, if she hadn't hired that devil," Robin said between clenched teeth. "I wouldn't have had to leave."

"After how she ruined your career," I said with a sympathetic nod. "I can understand."

"You have no idea." She halted so fast that I almost slammed into her, making the dog growl again.

I gentled my voice. "Tell me about it."

She shook her head, sending the curls of her wig writhing. "I've put it behind me."

Clearly, she hadn't.

"The day Devan disappeared, I was in Concord," Robin said

with such venom that it stung my cheeks. "My mother had taken me to the hospital for an involuntary psych eval."

I didn't get to ask any more questions, because that's when Page, who'd lagged behind, yelled and rolled down the trail.

9

We sat at the urgent care in Stoneley, waiting for someone to look at the wrist and ankle Page had sprained in her fall. A garland of jack-o-lanterns surrounded the waiting room. A spider and her web decorated the corner of the TV silently playing some sort of renovation show. A baseball-size pumpkin sat on a nest of red and orange maple leaves at the receptionist's window. As if all that fake fall cheer could hide the antiseptic smell and the anxiety permanently imprinted in the walls.

I called Evie to check on her and Harlan and told her where we were. I didn't want to talk to Harlan right now and get a lecture about minding my own business. The department was already strapped for officers, especially with two down. This is what I could do to help both Harlan and Owen.

Then while Page and I waited, we went over the information we'd gathered so far.

Devan had spent the first six weeks of school hurting people—Anji Parra (her supposed best friend), Oliver Taylor (her supposed boyfriend), Brent Benson (her patsy), Camden (her rival for the number one class spot), Robin Crawford (a teacher who wouldn't let her slide), the cheerleader she'd tripped on purpose to get a trick she'd wanted to perform herself, the student whose science project she'd sat on because it was better than hers. She'd most likely done more things that weren't reported; she was just that type of girl.

"What happened to her to make her so mean?" I asked.

"Have you seen her parents?" Page snorted. "She probably learned as a toddler that was the only way to get her parents' attention. She's not happy, Ellie, and she takes it out on everyone else. The problem is that you can't get your happiness from others, you have to find it for yourself."

Page should know. She'd had a hard start into adulthood with her parents dying six months apart, then being left at the altar.

As we chatted, I reordered my notes into a timeline. "Devan disappeared from the football game at halftime."

"We found her bones in the wall between my shop and Lillian's. Do you think they've been there for ten years?"

That was a question I hadn't considered. We couldn't look at the walls to see if decomposition fluids had soaked into the insulation and wall material because they were all gone now. When had the bones been stuffed between the walls? That same day or later? "Devan worked for Lillian. Lillian fired her because of the way she treated customers. She might not have killed Devan, but she might have helped Brent hide the fact he had."

I ticked each name on my list with the tip of a pen. "Brent Benson, Jason Parra, Oliver Taylor, and Robin Crawford all had a strong motive to want to hurt the girl who, by everyone's account, was not a nice person."

"Every year, she used to come to the Trick-or-Treat Extravaganza dressed as a witch," Page said. "Makes me wonder if she knew that about herself."

"I doubt it." I focused back on my notes. "Only Oliver Taylor had no alibi for halftime. But was that enough time to find someone, kill them and hide their body? Yet, Oliver's the only one to flee rather than face questions. What does he have to hide?"

"And how do we find out?" Page rubbed her lower leg.

"The rest of Devan's classmates either had solid alibis or were caught on the tape Alex Powers had filmed of the game for his college application."

I circled round and round and nothing stood out in neon, saying *I did it!*

Page lifted her swollen wrist. "Don't forget to add that someone tripped me."

"Are you sure?"

"That branch didn't magically appear on the trail."

Except that Page wasn't focused on where she was going but on the conversation. "Either we or the Paynes' private detective spooked someone enough to—" *Kill Owen and hurt Harlan.* Harlan, who took every occasion to ask questions, whether he was officially running the investigation or not. That was just who he was. His family and his community were everything to him.

I scrunched my eyes closed and forced myself to focus back on the bones.

"I have to find out what Harlan was working on before the accident." I swallowed hard, pushing back down the stampede waiting to sprint.

Page winced as she shifted her ankle. "Good luck getting him to share."

A nurse came through the door. "Page?"

"Hi, Lynette," Page said, struggling to get up even with my help.

"What did you do this time?" Lynette shook her head. Her dainty name didn't fit her wall-of-muscle body, or her coral scrubs dotted with cartoon dogs wearing Halloween costumes.

"I went hiking." Page could have a frequent-user card for the urgent care, as klutzy as she was.

Lynette's laugh sounded part growl. "Whatever possessed you?"

"I like to try new things."

"Well, stop it!" She ushered Page through the door, taking over supporting Page as she hop-limped.

Page stopped and waved at me. "Come with."

I'd looked forward to sitting by myself for a bit, but she was probably right. Sitting, my mind would turn to Harlan and Owen and poor Evie, and that was asking for trouble. Someone Harlan knew had killed Owen. On purpose. How was that even possible?

I sat in a corner chair in the cubicle. Lynette took down Page's information while Page peppered her with questions. "Did Brent Benson come in last Tuesday?"

"I see a lot of people, Page."

"He's the manager at the Shaw's. Fell at work."

"I wasn't working Tuesday, but I heard all about the fool who drove himself here instead of accepting an ambulance ride to the ER." She tsked. "Driving with a concussion."

"He drove himself?" I said, half rising from my chair. Was it possible? Could he have hit Harlan and Owen on his way to urgent care? He'd have had to go out of his way, down to Brighton, then back up to Stoneley, which didn't make sense. But it was the perfect cover to hide his intent. My nerve endings tingled. Had he fallen on purpose? How would he know where Harlan would be? Was Harlan even his target? Was it supposed to have been Lander?

"Between you and me, I heard he couldn't see straight." Lynette talked as she checked boxes on her computer. "Drove his car right up on the curb. Then left it there, running."

"What kind of car?" I asked, sinking back into the chair, dread twirling and twining like a poisoned weed.

Lynette gave me a puzzled look. "What does it matter?"

"What time was that?" Page's face had gone bloodless.

"I'm not sure. One-ish?"

Half an hour after someone rammed into Harlan and Owen. Long enough to get back to Stoneley.

"A black car?" I asked.

Lynette shrugged. "Could be. Like I said. I wasn't here."

I stared at Page. One o'clock. Right after someone hit Harlan and Owen and kept on driving. Left them there. Broken and bleeding.

Tears flowed down Page's face.

"What's happening?" Lynette's gaze ping-ponged from Page to me.

"Har-lan," Page blurted. "He almost died."

"Oh, I'm so sorry." Lynette propped a hip next to Page on the examining table and held her while she cried.

"Could Brent have hurt—?" Page chuffed out.

Brent had more than hurt Harlan. He'd stolen Owen away from his family, from his community. A man who just wanted to serve and protect Brighton.

"The time fits," I managed to say, imagining Harlan again, hurt on the side of the road in the rain.

That only made Page sob harder.

We'd taken Brent off the suspect list.

I put him back on at the number one spot.

"I can't stay home," Page said, hands knotted in her lap in the driveway of my house, staring at the red front door—a leftover from my Feng Shui phase. "I could use the company."

I nodded. "You can spend the night in Remy's room."

"Thank you."

Page, her right foot unhurt, drove her batmobile back home to get a change of clothes and toiletries. I took Stella Luna out. I checked on both Harlan and Evie. I stuffed a casserole from the freezer into the fridge to defrost.

Once Page was back, she made a vat of popcorn while I stirred together hot cider.

Evie padded into the living room wearing a green Hocus-Pocus sweatshirt that matched the color of her eyes and pumpkin-colored yoga pants. She'd dragged along a plush blanket that reminded me of the blankie she'd loved to pieces, literally, as a child.

"What's this?" Evie asked, plopping onto the sofa. The file from our investigation Page had left on the coffee table staring back at us.

"Notes." I gathered the file and stuffed it in a tote.

Evie frowned and tightened the blanket around her shoulders. "Mom, you have to stop this."

"It's fine, Bug." I handed her a pumpkin-shaped mug of steaming cider.

"No, it's not!" She held the mug with both hands, fingertips white against the orange ceramic sides. "I know how you are. Once you get hold of a bone, you can't let go. Like when someone stole my flute and you interrogated the whole fifth grade. Or when the cash box disappeared from Cammy's charity sale and you hunted down the two boys who took it all the way to Hopewell. Or when Remy lost Uncle Remy's watch and you looked under every rock of the park."

I'd been so angry at Remy for losing my dead brother's watch. She was right; I couldn't let go. I had to see things to their ends. A fault that had plagued me all my life. And now, no matter what, I had to find out why someone would want to take Harlan away from those who loved him.

From me.

Tears, like fat pearls, rolled down Evie's cheeks. "I can't lose anybody else right now."

That hit me like a punch to the gut. I didn't care what happened to me. But I also hadn't thought how my digging into this mess would affect my children, especially Evie.

"She's got me," Page said, settling in next to Evie and putting her good arm around Evie's shoulders, drawing her close. "I'll make sure your mom stays safe."

Evie nodded toward Page's wrapped ankle propped on a pillow. "Sorry, Aunt Page, but that's really not a comfort." She dropped her head on Page's shoulder. "Plus, I don't want to lose you either."

"You won't."

Once Evie had settled, we sat squashed on the couch, popcorn and cider on the coffee table, and watched the whole *The Good Witch* series. The casserole remained untouched in the fridge.

Somewhere late in the night—I should say early in the morning—we fell asleep.

I woke up to my phone blaring a warning. A notification flashed that an intruder had entered my home.

Heart beating a marathon, I slid Evie's head off my shoulder and onto a pumpkin pillow. Stella, sleeping with Harlan, ignored the intrusion. Some guard dog!

While I stepped into my shoes, I called 9-1-1, who told me that an officer was already on the way. Noises came from Harlan's office.

Who? Why?

I shook Page and Evie awake and sent them out the front door. "Shh. There's someone inside the house." I met Page's worried gaze. "Get in your car and drive to your house. Keep Evie safe. I'll call you."

"But—" Page started.

"Just do it, please."

For once, Page didn't fight a request. She wrapped an arm around Evie and led her out the front door. I tiptoed to the office door but didn't open it to confront the intruder. Someone was definitely in there. I kept going until I reached our bedroom. That's when Stella erupted with a flurry of barks, racing to Harlan's office.

"What's going on?" Harlan asked, groggy from the pain pills.

"Someone's in your office. Page took Evie to her place. Help's on the way."

Harlan scrambled up, reaching for his crutches and his service weapon.

"No," I said. "You can barely stand. Let Lander handle it."

Speaking of the devil, Lander walked in the front door, service weapon drawn. From the bedroom door, I pointed toward Harlan's office.

"Stay right there," he whispered.

An order, not a request.

He rubbed me the wrong way. Always had for some reason. But like Harlan, I would trust him with my life. Like Harlan, he'd devoted his life to protecting Brighton. He'd never married or had a relationship that lasted more than a few months. Though he was taller and broader than Harlan, I'd always thought he lacked Harlan's substance.

I'd promised Evie I wouldn't take chances, so I nodded and stayed put.

What seemed like an eternity later, but was only about a minute, according to my watch, Lander appeared at the office door and waved me in.

The office faced the backyard, away from the prying eyes of neighbors. A cold breeze fluttered through the open window, the obvious point of entry. Chaos awaited. Every drawer and file folder gaped open, emptied, as if whoever had rummaged through the office was looking for something specific.

"Is there anything missing?" Lander asked, watching me closely with his closeted gaze, a gaze that somehow made me want to squirm.

"I have absolutely no idea." I turned in place, taking in the utter destruction. "Who would do this? Why?"

"Have you been asking questions again? After you were specifically told to leave the investigating to the professionals?"

He was treating me like a naughty child. Anger was better than tears. "I can't help it if people talk to me."

I bent down to neaten the space.

"Leave it," Lander said. "I need to photograph first."

I nodded. "Right."

Proper procedures.

"Was the alarm system armed?" His eagle gaze drilled into me.

I turned away. "That's how you got notified. Whoever broke into the office didn't care that there was a houseful of people or that they'd triggered an alarm."

"That worries me."

The comment seemed so out of place for Lander that I stared at him over my shoulder.

"What?" he asked.

I shook my head, gave the mess one last look. That's when I caught sight of a piece of a photo Harlan had taken after we found the bones. I scoured the rest of the mess.

"The bone pictures are missing," I said, realizing there should be more than just that one corner of the bag.

Lander made a noise that he'd heard me and squatted next to the pile of ripped papers to examine them.

"I want to see the photos," I said, girding for battle.

"No." Just a single word with no give.

"I will with or without your permission."

That hard golden look again, as if he could see right through me. He stood up to his full height—one that had him ducking door frames on a regular basis—and gave a sharp nod. "You can't go exploring on your own."

I closed my eyes, my whole body stiffened, knowing that I couldn't stop even if I wanted to.

10

We all spent Sunday together, making sure Evie got through the weekend. On Monday morning, Evie insisted on going back to work. She needed the children, she said. Their smiles would be her best medicine, so I let her go, even though I wanted to hold her tight.

Harlan, too, insisted on getting up and hobbling to work. I drove him there and ordered him not to leave his desk. At least with the cast all the way up his leg, he couldn't drive. I told him to call when he wanted a ride home.

Once back home, I remembered that the printer in Harlan's office had a memory. Even though Lander had said he'd let me see the bone photos, I was one hundred percent sure he'd drag his feet as long as he could. So, I printed a set of photos from the printer memory.

I showered and changed into khakis and one of my better sweaters—one Page had knitted for me, with purple and black bats flying against a lavender background.

"We're going to work," I told Page, who was fussing over a pot of coffee.

"I was going to stay closed today," Page said, offering me my favorite stoneware mug.

"Do you have access to the apartment above the store?"

Page rummaged through the purple backpack she used as a purse, embroidered with *Something Wicked This Way Comes* on the flap. She dangled a leather bat keychain. "I have keys, but I've never used them."

"Let's."

"WE'VE LOOKED at the people around Devan's disappearance," I told Page once we'd arrived at the bookshop, Stella Luna at our heels. "But we haven't looked at the place."

The workers hadn't yet arrived on this Monday morning, but they soon would, so our window to explore was short. Already, they'd built the arch that would link the café with the bookshop, erasing the hole Page had made. The scent of sawdust and primer filled the air. I could make out the skeleton of the kitchen. I couldn't see how all the work would get done in less than two weeks.

I took off Stella's leash and let her wander. Tail wagging in a slow arc, she sniffed and sniffed.

"We should go to the high school, too," Page said, trying each key in turn. "Scope out the landscape. See if there's some place the killer could've stashed Devan before he put her in the wall."

Remy had graduated from the Tri-Town High School three years ago, so I wasn't as familiar with its layout as I once was. "Good idea."

The door leading to the upstairs apartment creaked. The narrow stairs lacked proper lighting, and shadows stretched into hazards. The air smelled of neglect. Stella and her curious nose added an extra obstacle to our climb.

"Maybe you should stay down here," I said to Page. "We don't want another trip to urgent care."

She gripped both sides of the rails and hopped up on the first step. "No way!"

At the top of the staircase, we found two doors. Page fumbled with the keys again and opened the door above Lillian's shop. It, too, squealed as if it hadn't seen any activity in a decade instead of a month and a half.

Page turned on the light. Soft light showered the room that seemed frozen in time. Along the back wall, three angled floor-to-ceiling mirrors reflected a circular stage. Stella had a field day with all the foreign scents.

"I didn't think Lillian sold wedding dresses," I said, taking in the velvet couch, once raspberry now grayed with dust, the antique white armoire where dresses once hung, and the Aubusson rug in pinks and teals that gave the place the feel of a cozy den. A silver tray with a china tea set rested on top of a mini-fridge. Getting a dress fitted here would feel like pampering.

Page hobbled onto the stage and twirled like an out-of-whack top. "She didn't have many wedding dresses, but she sold a few over the years. Jenna Cooper, for one. She did a lot of proms, though. And gala dresses."

Both Cammy and Evie had insisted they needed a trip to Boston to shop for their prom dresses. We'd made a day out of it and had fun, one-on-one mother-daughter time, even though Cammy ended up never going to her prom.

"I don't think I've ever been in this side before." Page hobbled off the stage and snooped in various nooks and crannies, Stella following her every step in case Page uncovered something interesting.

"Me either." The store had seemed too frou-frou. I liked simple, soft clothes. Like Evie, I had sensitive skin and had to cut labels out of my clothes.

I studied the wall that shared Page's side of the building. I found no tell-tale signs of tampering. But who knew, maybe the murderer had an affinity for drywall repair. I tried to move the armoire, but even with Page's help, the heavy wooden furniture wouldn't budge. Someone would have to be strong to move it on their own. Which eliminated all our suspects, except maybe Oliver. Unless, of course, more than one person was involved.

"Let's go look next door." I sighed. I'd hoped to find obvious signs that a crime had taken place.

Page unlocked the other door. Stella wriggled through first. The lighting here was starker, illuminating a cutting table, a sewing table with an old Singer sewing machine, and a wall of bookcases filled with sewing supplies, which conveniently hid the wall between the apartments. Boxes were piled onto a hand truck, backed against the wall. Two rolling racks flanked each side of the sewing table, one marked In and the other Out.

I wandered through the room, trailing a hand through the dust. "You'd think that Lillian would want this stuff or at least want to sell it."

Page was lost in her own world. "I wonder if I could lease this space as a reading room or a meeting room."

"Isn't the café going to add enough to your lease?"

She waved my comment away. "It'll take care of itself. I always wanted to have a space where writers could meet. An old-fashioned salon." She created a frame with her hands, as if she held a camera, and panned the room. "Along that wall, I could have offices writers could rent. Here, a library filled with reference books. There, couches for reading." She dropped her hands. "It's too bad there isn't a fireplace. That would be the icing on the writers' space."

"You think there are enough writers in the area to make that a viable idea?"

She shrugged a shoulder. "Everybody wants to write a book."

Including my two daughters. I had no such desire.

We exited the apartment, Stella leading the charge. Then I stopped, causing Page to wobble. "Look at this," I said, tracing the space between the walls. I had Page open both doors. "The walls between the apartments doesn't look right. When you stuck your head between the walls, how much space was there?"

"I could put my whole head in no problem."

"I wonder why?" Most normal walls had what, six inches of space between them? This one looked at least a foot wide. "Let's go back downstairs."

I studied the arch. "Look at how wide it is. No wonder a whole body in a gym bag fit in there."

"For extra insulation?" Page asked.

"Did whoever kill Devan know about the wall?"

"Had to."

"It's too bad we can't ask the original architect."

"But we can ask a builder." Page pointed to the curb where Aaron Carpenter parked his red truck in front of the bookstore.

Aaron was kind enough to oblige our questions about the wall. "There's piping in there. A flue."

"You mean that at some point there was a fireplace in here?" Page's face brightened like a kid who was just offered a triple-decker sundae.

"Or a woodstove," Aaron said.

We hadn't seen a woodstove upstairs and neither shop had had one.

Page, no doubt dreaming of her writers' space, hooked her arm through Aaron's elbow. "Come with me. There's something I want to show you."

∾

WHILE PAGE TROUBLED Aaron with her pipe dream, I headed to
the high school to take Stella for a walk and look around.

School was in session, so the parking lot was filled, and I
had to park on the street. I sat on the bleachers, imagining that
day—the game, which also happened to be one of the area's
biggest rivalries, my girls in their band uniforms, catching sight
of Harlan patrolling the crowd, the halftime show I'd almost
missed because Remy had wandered off and I'd had to go
retrieve him before he got in trouble.

The Tri-Town school complex consisted of a high school, a
middle school and an elementary school all together in a hub
in more or less the center where all three towns met. Which
meant it was in the middle of nowhere. Sports fields, a playground and two parking lots ringed the buildings. Woods
surrounded three sides of the complex. Although, technically,
the school campus was closed, Brighton didn't have the
manpower to have a resource officer stationed at the school
complex. No one would stop me from wandering outside.

I headed toward the spot in the far end of the student lot
where Devan's car was found. Stella grabbed a stick the size of
a wrist, dropped it at my feet, and barked until I threw it for her.
She loved a good game of fetch.

Cars used up every single space available—just like they
would have on that day. Several trails led into the woods where
I found squashed cigarette butts and empty beer cans.

"Drop it!" I said to Stella, who had picked up a butt. She spit
it out and parked at my feet for a treat. I dug into my pocket and
found a piece of dog jerky.

I swiveled around and Stella went back to exploring. These
trails would make it easy to stash a body to move later. But ten
years had long ago erased any evidence, if there'd been any to
find. I whistled. "Stella, come!"

Stella didn't magically appear with a piece of evidence in
her mouth. That would have been too easy.

I sighed and hooked Stella's leash back on her harness. "Let's go home."

I was driving through Stoneley's main street when I spotted what looked like Oliver Taylor's Jeep—silver with blue trim. I recognized the Appalachian Trail bumper stickers and the tires with the deep grooves meant to handle mud. How many Jeeps with that exact color scheme could exist in two small towns?

So, I followed him.

All the way to the north end of Manchester, right across from downtown to an apartment building with views of the Merrimack River. He wormed around the side of the building where someone waited to let him into the parking garage.

Someone that looked suspiciously like Anji Parra.

FOR AN APARTMENT whose monthly rental fee had to top our mortgage payment, it lacked in security. No front desk. No security guard. A bank of mailboxes, conveniently labeled with the renters' last names.

Anji lived on the top floor in one of the four "penthouse" apartments. Stella at my side, I knocked on her door.

She frowned when she saw me. "Mrs. Hamlin? What are you doing here?"

"I need to talk to both you and Oliver."

"Oliver who?" Anji asked innocently.

"I saw you let his Jeep into the garage."

"It's okay," came Oliver's voice from inside. "Let her in."

Anji spotted Stella. "It's a no-pet building."

"We won't stay long."

Oliver looked like a wreck, hair unkempt as if he'd run his hands through it so many times that it was easier for it to stand up than to lie in its usual style. Dark purple circles rimmed his eyes. He sat on the edge of the beige leather couch, elbows on knees, hands holding up his head.

"Anji's helping me," Oliver said before I had a chance to sit down.

Stella, ever sensitive to human emotions, gently placed her head on Oliver's lap.

"Why?" I asked, taking a seat in the chair across from him. Anji sat beside him, rubbing his back.

"He didn't do it," Anji said. "But the evidence is stacked against him. It doesn't look good."

"How do you know he didn't do it?"

Her cheeks pinkened. "He was on the phone with me when Devan disappeared."

"That didn't show up in his phone records."

Oliver patted Stella's head. "The coach locked up our phones during practices and games. Wanted us to have our full focus on the play. I had to borrow a phone from some random person in the crowd."

"Why were you calling Anji?"

His gaze met mine. "To warn her."

"About?"

"Devan was on a tear." Anji straightened the already perfectly placed file on the glass coffee table. "She was angry."

"Why did you run after we chatted?" I asked as his body relaxed, thanks to Stella.

"The bones in my bag doesn't look good. I knew the cops would finger me as the prime suspect, even though I played the whole game."

I tilted my head. "You did disappear at halftime."

He hugged Stella. "When I got to the locker room, my bag was gone."

"You suspected Devan had taken it," I said.

He nodded. "I went after her. Got to her right as she was

starting her car. My bag was right there in her back seat. I ordered her to give it back to me. She laughed, threw the car in reverse. She would've run me over if I hadn't moved out of the way."

He raked both hands through his hair and pressed his fingertips against his nape. "She had such hatred in her eyes. She knew I liked Anji. And she knew Anji liked me. She was no longer the most important person to us. I was afraid she'd take it out on Anji. Again."

"Because you two were seeing each other," I said.

"Not exactly." Anji glanced at Oliver with softness. "I was living with my grandparents in Belmont at the time. We were just talking. It helped after..."

"What Devan did to you." I turned my attention back to Oliver. "So, you warned Anji and..."

"I had no choice." Stella pawed at his knee, and he scratched her ears. "I went back to the locker room and played the second half."

Which Alex Powers had caught on tape.

"But why run now, Oliver?" I asked. "Anji can back up your story."

Anji's glance went to the file on the table. "The circumstantial physical evidence counts more than my word."

"You took a risk leaving Angi's apartment," I said to Oliver. "Why?"

"I'd paid Alex Powers to tape me during the fall games to help with my college applications. Maybe something on there could point me to the right person." He looked at Anji and his whole body relaxed. "Especially now, because—"

"You've reconnected."

They both nodded.

"And this..." Anji reached into the file and brought out a photo of Oliver arguing with Devan on that day ten years ago.

"Where did it come from?"

"It's from a number I didn't recognize, and the Brighton PD was on the joint text."

Just like that video, showing Camden arguing with Devan.

"Have you ever been to the apartments above the bookshop?"

Oliver closed his eyes, hands woven at his nape, curling over himself like a turtle trying to shrink back into its shell. Stella licked his face, but he didn't seem to notice. "Miss Crawford tutored me senior year. I needed to bring my math grades up to stay on the team. And I needed to stay on the team to go to college."

Another thing that wouldn't play in his favor.

Because if he'd been in the apartment, he may have known about the wall.

11

W
ith both Harlan and Evie at work, I didn't want to go to my empty home. I didn't want to go to Page's shop either. I didn't want her bright chirp in my ear as she spouted on about her new ideas for the upstairs apartments. She always went overboard. I needed grounding in reality, not a flight of fancy. I needed to keep moving. Fool that I was, I ended up on the road where the accident had taken place.

The mud on the shoulder had dried, leaving deep ruts where the car had rammed into Harlan, Owen and the teen's car. Small shards of taillights winked in the sun like red sequins. I crouched, touched the earth that had drunk Owen and Harlan's blood. Just a few inches had made a difference between life and death.

Though I felt sorry for Owen's parents, I was also grateful Harlan was spared. Like a film on a screen, our life together played. Harlan smiling at me. Harlan holding me. Harlan loving me. With him I was safe. We'd made a good life together. That was enough. That was my happy.

Slow tears spilled down my cheeks. Stella whined and

barked and scratched at the window inside the car. How could something like this happen in beautiful Brighton? What if I'd lost Harlan just like the McGills had lost Owen?

Tires crunching on the gravel shoulder made me look up. Lander unfolded from his car. Of course, he'd show up to see me at my worst.

He crouched next to me, reached a hand to help me sit up. "What are you doing here?"

The gentleness in his voice, in his strange golden eyes, seemed out of place with his usual gruffness.

"I had to see." I had to feel. I had to know. I'd come so close to losing Harlan.

Lander handed me a handkerchief. I wiped the tears from my cheeks. "What are *you* doing here?"

"We had a report of someone crying by the side of the road."

"So naturally, you decided to come to the rescue."

He held on to my arm until we both stood. "I just wanted to make sure you were okay."

"I'm fine." I dusted dirt from the sleeve of my bat sweater. I didn't need his pity. Voice cracking like glass, I asked, "What's going on with the case?"

"You know I can't talk about it."

I stood, ignoring the dirt on my khakis, staring at the ground. "Your choice, of course."

"Ellie..." He shook his head and, for a moment, I thought I saw a speck of vulnerability. I'd almost lost the love of my life. But he'd lost a fellow officer and almost lost his best friend. One he'd had since grade school.

Stiff as if someone had doused me with starch, I headed for the car and reached for the door handle. I'd started this. I couldn't stop. If I did this for Harlan, for Evie, for Owen, then maybe the guilt would go away. Throat tight, I said, "Who's watching out so Harlan doesn't do too much?"

"Micah and I are taking shifts."

"I have to know." I begged him to understand.

Lander heaved a sigh. "We've put out a warrant for Oliver Taylor's arrest."

Poor Oliver. Even with Anji's help, he had a long road ahead of him before he could prove his innocence. "As usual, you got it wrong."

I slid into the seat and slammed the door shut. Stella barked and wagged her tail, demanding Lander's attention.

"So, if you're so smart, who did it?" he asked through the closed window, one elbow leaning on the roof.

"Still working out the logistics." I turned on the ignition, cranked on the heat. Then I roared away in the opposite direction, leaving him standing on the side of the road.

The tracks, I thought, remembering the dried ruts. They'd come from Brighton, not Stoneley. I made a U-turn and went back in the direction from which the murder car had come.

Twice, I went back to the spot where someone had mowed down Owen and Harlan. Twice the trajectory didn't seem quite right.

On the third try, where the road curved and the shoulder widened for a trailhead, I found the correct angle. The car had been waiting there. Why? How could someone possibly know that Harlan would be there?

I dialed Lander's number. "The murder car was waiting for Harlan and Owen at the Mt. Hope trailhead off Mountain Road."

"I know."

Hands gripping the steering wheel as if it could keep me grounded, I asked, "Did you take a cast of the tire tracks?"

"You know, Ellie, this isn't my first investigation."

"Mine either." I'd spent so many evenings, sitting in the kitchen, Harlan's sounding board as he went through the puzzle pieces of an investigation.

Lander sighed again as if I were a thorn in his side. "We figure that someone caused the flat tire that sent Harlan and Owen to the teen. There was an anonymous call, reporting the incident."

Someone had willfully caused this young woman's accident. Someone had deliberately called the police to the scene. My throat and lungs hurt from the weight of my guilt. "Man or woman?"

"Hard to tell. It sounded like they had a bad cold."

"You couldn't trace the call."

"Burner phone."

"That didn't seem odd to you?" The horizon spun in dizzying arcs. Who would want to hurt Harlan or Owen on purpose?

"Ellie, really, I've got this. Harlan's my best friend. Someone's going to pay for killing Owen and hurting Harlan."

On that point, I believed him. He would try to get justice for Owen and Harlan.

But he had rules to follow.

And I didn't.

I DROVE BACK to the bookshop, leaving Stella in the car with the window open. I would only be gone for a few minutes. The workers had left for the day. No customer lingered this close to closing time. Page sat at the front counter, smiling like a fool at a piece of paper in front of her.

"There you are," Page said, holding the piece of printer paper by the edges, showing off a design that matched her vision for the upstairs. "What do you think?"

"Wow, it's as if Aaron somehow got right in that weird brain of yours and drew your idea on paper."

"I know." Her smile widened. "Isn't it great?"

I leaned both elbows on the desk. "So, you're going to do it?"

"I have to run it by the landlord first, but yeah, I want to. I can see it already, a literary center, right here in Brighton."

"I think that maybe you should study the area's demographics before you go through the expense."

She laid the paper on the counter and smoothed it. "'If you build it, he will come.'"

"Not sure how manifesting a baseball player is going to help your cause."

Page laughed. "Ye of little faith."

"You look like that ankle's hurting. Have you been elevating it like Lynette told you to?"

Still staring at her dream, she shrugged. "I've been busy."

"Go home," I said and grabbed the bat keychain that held the store keys. "I'll lock up."

She nodded and slid off her stool. "Where were you all day?"

"Around."

"Find any clues?"

"More like they're all jumbling together and not making sense."

Page nodded. "Maybe we should let Lander do his job."

I snorted. "He's arresting Oliver Taylor."

"Maybe he's right. Maybe you're wrong this time." She grabbed her backpack, slid it over her shoulders and headed for the door. "See you at your house in a bit."

UPSTAIRS, in the stairwell between the two apartment doors, I studied the span of the wall. The width still bothered me. Neither Lillian's side of the wall nor Page's side showed signs of tampering. Or signs of ever having had a fireplace. Unless the fireplace wasn't on this floor.

I went back to the main floor and studied the wall and the floor. The arch had taken away a good chunk of wall, but Aaron hadn't encountered the flue there. Which meant it had to be closer to the back wall, because who would put a fireplace right at the entrance?

I headed for the basement. In the first house Harlan and I had shared, the basement had a woodstove that was supposed to heat the house in case of a power failure. All it ever did was belch smoke all over the house.

I should have figured this out by now.

Yeah, right! If the police couldn't figure out where Devan had gone for ten years, what made me think I could solve the mystery of her murder in a few weeks?

Maybe Lander was right. Maybe I should stop sticking my nose into what was none of my business.

Except that Harlan was my business. And I needed to know why this happened to him. I needed to make sense of this madness. I needed to feel safe in my own town again.

I spotted the old woodstove a quarter of the way down the wall separating Lillian and Page's shops, closest to the back. A black cast-iron beast, almost hidden by the staircase's shadow. It looked as if it hadn't worked in decades. The wood hopper was empty. I craned my neck to look at where the flue joined the ceiling.

I raced back up the stairs, crossed the quiet street and studied the roofline, Stella barking at me from the car. A redbrick chimney sat square toward the back end of the roof. Why hadn't I noticed it before? Not that it mattered. The facts of the stove and the chimney didn't help in understanding how Devan had ended up in the space between the walls—only why the space between the walls was so wide.

Sighing, I went back inside to close. As much as I hated to

admit it, I needed a good night's sleep. I reached for the light switch leading to the basement.

Two palms collided with my shoulder blades.

"You were warned," said a voice that sounded rusty.

With an *oomph*, I went cascading down the steps. I tucked and rolled, but still landed hard on the concrete floor. This was how I was going to die, I thought. Like a bug squashed under someone's shoe.

I'd promised Evie I wouldn't die. That I wouldn't break her heart all over again. I couldn't die. Not this way. I rolled onto my back, heart beating like a time bomb, breath like a freight train. My left side pulsed like one giant bruise. My shoulder smarted. My knee screamed. Would whoever had pushed me come down and finish the job?

Stay quiet, I told myself, holding my breath, lungs burning. I forced my eyes to stay closed. *Let whoever pushed you think you're dead.*

I slit an eye open, peering up the staircase into the darkened store. A swish of black raced across the opening like a knight heading into battle.

The door clanged shut and the lights sparked out.

I bit back an involuntary squeal.

When the shop's front door slammed shut, I puffed out a breath.

Head ringing, shaking all over like an aspen in autumn, I scrambled up, arms braced in a pitiful boxing stance, just in case the black knight returned to finish the job. Why hadn't they?

If I get out of here alive, I promised, *I'll give Lander everything I have and let him take care of it.*

Every muscle in my body aching, shaking my head to disrupt the ringing, I patted my pocket. No phone. I'd left it in my purse in the car with Stella.

Holding the railing with one hand and the other palm flat

against the stairwell, I climbed up the stairs. I turned the knob and jiggled it to no avail. Of course, the door was locked. Of course, the lock was on the outside. And, of course, the light switch wouldn't turn on, no matter how hard I flipped the thing.

I sat on the top stair, rubbing my sore temples. *Think, Ellie, think! Before the lights went out, what did you see?*

I'd focused on the woodstove. That would offer no exit. I let my gaze wander through the night-black room, picturing what was there when the lights were on. A pile of furniture at the far end—a discarded kitchen table and chairs, a bureau, a broken-down bed frame. From the apartments upstairs? Boxes of different sizes. I could use all that to climb. Only one problem. No windows. Of course not. Escaping couldn't be that easy.

"The workbench!" Tucked in the back corner, it held an assortment of neglected tools.

I made my way down the stairs again, then across the concrete floor, taking small steps, tamping the air with my hands in front of me to avoid bumping into anything. I still managed to knock my knee on the leg of the workbench. "Buttered bananas!"

Before kids, I'd had a potty mouth. I hadn't wanted them to share that inclination, so I'd made up funny expressions. Buttered bananas was Remy's favorite.

I gave my knee a quick rub to ease the sting, then blindly searched the workbench top for something with which to break open the door. I discarded screwdrivers, pliers, then landed on a hammer. "Yes!"

I climbed up the stairs as fast as I dared.

That's when I smelled the smoke. They hadn't needed to kill me up close because they were planning on doing it with fire.

"No, no, no!" The books. Page's babies. They would burn

fast. I'd be dead from smoke inhalation before anyone even realized the shop was on fire.

I battered the lock with all my strength, taking all my frustrations out against it. An eternity later, it broke apart. Coughing, I pulled my sweater over my nose and headed to the checkout counter where I called 9-1-1.

I found Page's fire extinguisher and aimed it at the flames eating away at the tarps the workers had left behind. I doused the flames with foam. I'd caught the fire fast enough that it hadn't caused much damage, except for scorching the wood flooring under the tarps. It would give Page a story to regale her customers.

Movement fluttered outside the shop. A black car pulled away from the curb across the street. A car a teenager might describe as old-fashioned. I'd seen that car before.

Coughing, I scrambled outside to my car. Stella, tail wagging, attempted to lick my face, but her seat belt held her back. I had several messages from Harlan. I couldn't deal with a phone call, so I texted Evie and asked her if she could pick up her father. Once the sirens blared from the fire station, I drove away. I would give the police a statement later.

Right now, I needed to catch up with that car.

This late at night, the roads were empty, so I left my lights off and followed the black car. It wound through the streets of Brighton, first as if heading toward Lakeshore Drive, along Brighton Lake, home to the posher houses. Near the small airport, it slowed, giving me a chance to hide at the entrance to Candlewick Park. The car reversed and went back through town, along Wood Road toward Stoneley. Somewhere along the way, I lost track of the car. But that was okay. I knew exactly where I'd find it.

12

I rolled to a stop across the street from Lillian Watt's home. I petted Stella's soft head. "If I'm not back in five minutes, bark your head off."

Stella wagged her tail and tried to worm her way out of the car. "I'll be right back."

Making sure I had my cell phone with me this time, I trotted up to the garage. Both hands cupping the window, I peeked inside. Yep, right where I'd expected to see it, the black Pontiac GTO—my brother had a thing for cars, which meant I was decent at recognizing them—this time without a tarp. Lillian's white Lincoln sat parked right beside it.

I took a photo of the black car's plate—one that had expired thirteen years ago, according to the sticker. The year Lillian's husband had died. Then I sent Lander a text, outlining my theory, along with the photo.

I didn't wait for an answer. I hurried to the door and rang the doorbell. I needed answers before Lander shut me out.

Lillian, well put together as usual in her pressed black slacks, starched white blouse and beige knee-length cardigan, answered the door. Only her perfect platinum chignon was a tad askew. "Mrs. Hamlin, what are you doing here?"

Didn't expect to see me again, did you? "I have a few questions."

Her pale blue eyes turned to ice, but she opened the door wider. "Do come in. Would you like some tea?"

"That would be great."

I followed her to the kitchen, noticing the packing boxes in the darkened living room. "You're moving so soon?"

"I got a good offer on the house. And after my visit with my sister, we decided it would be best to share a home to avoid elder care for as long as possible. Given how the cold hurts my bones these days, we decided I should move to Florida."

"How nice for both of you." How convenient for Lillian to be far away when the truth came out. Too bad she wouldn't make it there.

I hovered by the kitchen door, watching her every move-ment as she filled the stainless-steel kettle and pulled two flowery teacups from a glass-fronted cupboard.

"A new start." Lillian's smile reminded me of a rabid dog's snarl.

She shuffled toward a pantry, hooked the silver head of her ebony cane over her forearm before entering, and came back out with a blue tin of shortbread cookies. "You had questions?"

"Just one. Why did you kill Owen?"

She tilted her head and gave me a pitying look. "It wasn't personal, dearie."

"It felt personal to the McGills. To me."

"He wasn't supposed to die. No one was. I didn't know that young man and your husband would answer the call. The acci-dent was meant as a distraction."

Killing a young man in cold blood and hurting another was a distraction? "What do you mean?"

She let go of the tin of cookies, which landed in a clatter on the floor, and jabbed her cane at my chest. "It was supposed to keep the police department focused on who hit one of their own rather than on Devan's bones."

Face taut, jaw tight, she pulled a gun from the pocket of her cardigan and waved it toward the pantry. "In you go."

When I didn't move, she whacked my shoulder with her cane, making me wince with pain. She shoved me forward.

Shoulder smarting, I lifted my hands in surrender. She stepped behind me, gun at my ribs to remind me she was armed. I took my time obeying her, scanning the path to the pantry for possible weapons. The knife block on the counter was too far. So was the electric kettle. The woman obviously didn't cook; her counters were much too clear. I bided my time until I reached the table with its fruit bowl piled with apples. "You killed Devan."

"So, what if I did?" She jabbed her cane between my shoulder blades to keep me moving forward. "You can't prove it."

With a sweep of my leg, I spun around and sent a kitchen chair skittering back into her legs. She lost her balance and toppled over onto her bad hip. She hit the floor with a crack. The gun went off, bullet piercing the ceiling and raining plaster between us.

I lunged toward her, aiming to disarm her.

She scrabbled back and two-handed the gun in my direction. "Take one more step and I will shoot."

I reached for the fruit bowl and launched it at the gun. Apples tumbled. The gun skittered under the table. Glass on the kitchen door shattered, tinkling to the floor. Lander and Micah burst in through the back door. "Police! Drop your weapon!"

LANDER INSISTED I see a doctor in the emergency room to make sure none of my injuries needed care. The same emergency room where an ambulance had taken Lillian and her newly rebroken hip. With orders to rest, I was discharged.

When Lander saw me, he rose from the orange plastic seat in the waiting room. "You shouldn't have confronted Lillian. If you suspected she killed Devan and Owen, you had to know she was dangerous."

I lifted a sore shoulder, regretted the move. "I had to know why she killed Owen and hurt Harlan."

He wrapped me in a quick hug. The warmth of his arms reminded me of Harlan's. Then Lander pointed me toward the sliding doors. "Micah dropped Stella off at home. Your car's in the lot. Go home. Be with Harlan. It's going to be a long night here."

I opened my mouth to protest, and he stopped me with a palm. "I promise I'll stop by after Lillian Watt is processed."

ONCE HOME, I'd had to listen to a lecture from Harlan. The worry on his face made me contrite. I'd fed Stella, taken her for a walk through the neighborhood. I took a long, hot shower, hoping it would allow me to sleep. It didn't. When staring at the ceiling got too frustrating, I got up, put on soft gray lounge pants and a green sweater that Harlan said brought out the color of my eyes. Not wanting to fall prey to nerves, I baked— pumpkin muffins, apple cider muffins, pecan streusel muffins. All the while, Stella watched my every step from her post by Harlan's feet. He'd fallen asleep on the recliner with the TV on.

Dawn purpled the morning sky before a tired and disheveled Lander knocked on my door, as promised. Harlan joined us at the kitchen table, resting his broken leg on an extra chair.

Cuffed to a hospital bed, before surgery for her shattered hip, Lillian had given a full confession.

"You were right," Lander said, sitting at my kitchen table, twirling a mug of coffee between his hands. "She killed both Devan and Owen."

"She told me that killing Owen was random—whoever answered the call would become her victim. A distraction—" My voice cracked, so I rose and grabbed a basket of muffins from the counter. I placed it in front of Lander, but he ignored it. "But why kill Devan?"

Lander wiped a hand across his haggard eyes. "She said Devan broke into her store during halftime. She'd made a copy of the key but didn't realize Lillian had changed the silent alarm code. When we didn't answer her call as fast as she liked, she decided to handle the matter herself. Before we could show up, she called it in as a false alarm."

"I remember that call," Harlan said. "We were too busy doing crowd control to answer."

"Why was Devan at the boutique?" I pulled the muffin cup away from a pumpkin muffin, giving it all my attention as if I were a surgeon.

Lander stared at the ceiling and got up. "Apparently, she was stealing another girl's prom dress. She forced Lillian to alter it for her at gunpoint."

"The red sequins," Harlan said, and tore his own muffin to pieces.

Lander nodded, disappeared into the garage and came back with a light bulb. "When Lillian jabbed her with a pin by mistake, Devan backhanded her. Lillian reacted by cracking her cane on her head."

"The hole in the skull."

Harlan lifted an eyebrow in question.

I shook my head in quick strokes. I wasn't about to tell him —or Lander—about the printer memory. "Not important."

With a hand, I urged Lander to continue his story. "She hit Devan with her cane."

Lander unscrewed the dead light bulb from the recessed fixture in the ceiling. "She said it was a reflex. That she didn't mean to kill her."

I glanced at the massacre of muffin in front of Harlan, wrapped the crumbs in the muffin cup, and pushed it away. So much death and for what? A slap from an unhappy girl who thought someone else's dress would make her happy? Owen had died because of a reflex from that slap? "How did Devan end up in the wall?"

Lander shook his head in a tired arc, removed the new bulb from its box and screwed it in place. "Lillian thought about putting Devan in her own car and leaving the car somewhere but found out how hard it is to move a dead body. When she couldn't dress her back into her own clothes, she somehow folded Devan into the duffel she found in Devan's car and shoved her between the walls. Later that night, she drove the car back to the high school student parking lot and walked back home."

"We'd looked for Devan's car," Harlan said. "It wasn't in the parking lot after the game."

I got up and scooped the muffin crumbs into the garbage can. "That's a lot of distance for a woman with a bum hip and a cane."

Lander placed the burnt bulb in the box. "Apparently, the cane was mostly for show. She said it helped her get commissions for accessible clothing."

She was definitely going to need it now. "I still don't get how she got in the wall. I saw no evidence of a hole."

Lander sat back down, box between his hands. "The fitting room wasn't quite finished, so it was easy enough to cut a hole in the wall, then use the law of gravity to dump her into the hole."

"The hand truck in the sewing room." I got up and refilled my coffee mug. "Who fixed the wall?"

Lander gave a derisive snort. "She's not afraid of technology. Or working with her hands. There are videos for everything online. She just followed the instructions on how to fix drywall, primed the wall and let the painters do the rest when they came back to finish the fitting room job the next Monday morning."

"I remember talking to her once about where she'd come from," Harlan said. "She grew up on a farm in Pennsylvania, so she knew about lime."

With a pensive look, Lander twirled the bulb box round and round. "The gun she used on you was registered to Calvin Payne—it was the gun Devan used to force Lillian to alter the dress."

"Wow." Who would have thought such a prim and proper little old lady could manage all that? "Did she send the video of Cammy and the photo of Oliver arguing with Devan?"

"I don't know where she found them or how she knew how to use a burner phone, but yeah, she did."

How could anyone be so cold-blooded? "I have a hard time believing she broke into our home."

"That was Brent," Harlan said. "We found his prints."

"He wanted to know what the police knew and figured he'd find out the easy way," Lander said. "Apparently, he suspected his grandmother all along and wanted to protect her."

Harlan scoffed. "He had to know I have a service weapon and know how to use it."

"Easier than the police department," Lander said. "And he knew you were hurt."

"She pushed me down the stairs at Page's bookshop." I kept my gaze anywhere but on Harlan. I hadn't yet told him about what had happened at the bookstore.

"She what?" Harlan asked, voice tight and thin.

I shook my head in quick strokes and waved his worry away. "Later." The cane had made her look like a knight brandishing a sword and that's when I'd remembered the shape of the hole in the photo of the skull. "She started the fire."

"You're lucky you didn't get hurt more than you did." Harlan's eyes narrowed, softened. "Ellie, I could've lost you."

Stella agreed with a whine.

He reached for my hand and squeezed it.

"I know." I was so focused on getting justice for Harlan and Owen that I forgot all I had to live for, all I already had that made me happy. "It won't happen again." I looked directly into Harlan's concerned eyes and squeezed his hand back. "I promise."

13

The bookshop looked magical with its over-the-top Halloween haunted house decorations. Haunting music poured through the speakers. Page had installed her life-size black coffin complete with skeleton for maximum spooky effect in the new café.

Platters of goodies from the Brightside Bakery—pumpkin cupcakes, bat-shaped sugar cookies and white-chocolate pretzel fingers with almond sliver nails—were displayed on the café tables. Cauldrons of candy popped up in unexpected places.

Elana Fisher, accompanied by her little therapy dog Marlie, read ghost stories in the new story time circle. Two dozen elementary school children sat with rapt attention and managed to forget temporarily about all the candy. A pack of older kids hovered close by, wanting to hear, yet feeling above sitting on the floor with the littles. Parents wandered the aisles, keeping an eye on their kids and gossiping about Lillian Watt and Devan's bones. Outside a crowd milled, going in and out of stores to collect candy booty.

The kitchen in the café still needed an inspection before it could officially open, but everything was in place—just as Page had predicted. Aaron and his crew had done good work.

Page, dressed in full witch costume, complete with green skin and fake wart on her nose, held court at the checkout counter. She'd dressed Stella Luna as a black cat familiar. I don't know how she got those cat ears to stick on Stella. I slid in beside Page to help.

"Everything looks great, Page." I placed a collection of Halloween board books into a bag while Page took payment.

"I told you everything would turn out."

"You did." I didn't know where Page got all her optimism, given all the disappointments she'd suffered, but I liked being around her positivity. Right now, I needed it. I needed the reminder to find joy in little things every day. To make my own happiness, the way she had. As this bones-in-the-wall experience had shown me, life was too short not to.

"Speaking of things turning out," I said. "Thanks for calling Lander when I didn't come back home."

"He was already on his way." Page's smile wobbled. "After he got your message. Plus, Harlan called him, too, when you sent Evie to pick him up."

I needed to accept things as they were and stop trying to make them fit to my expectations. I'd known Harlan was selfless before I married him. It was his best quality. Why had I expected him to change just because retirement loomed on the horizon?

The most important thing was love. And we shared an abundance of love.

"Harlan insisted on working tonight," I said with a small laugh, imagining Harlan on crutches out there somewhere in the milling crowd, keeping an eye on his Brightonian flock. As if on cue, the crowd parted and there he was. He caught my gaze, gave a smile, and went back to guardian mode.

"All those people to keep safe." Page leaned a head on my

shoulder, poking me with the pointy tip of her witch hat. "Sleuthing wasn't as fun as I thought it would be."

We'd almost paid too high a price.

"Next time, I'll listen to you," she said.

I chuckled. That promise would last until something caught her fancy and displaced logic. "Hopefully, there won't be another murder in Brighton for a long, long time."

* * *

THANK YOU FOR READING! While the story is fresh in your mind, I'd be eternally grateful if you took a few minutes to write a review. Your review helps more than you think. It would make my day.

ACKNOWLEDGMENTS

Thank you to everyone who had a hand in making this book come to life.

Lorrie Thomson, for the multiple, last-minute chapter re-reads.

My sister Joanne, a writer's dream fan.

The industry professionals who make this book beautiful: Bev Rosenbaum, Elaini Caruso and Christine of Open Book Design.

ABOUT THE AUTHOR

Sylvie started writing as a mom of two kids under four while living in a neighborhood with few stay-at-home moms. Feeling lonely and dying for conversation, she created characters and stories for company. She eventually succeeded, authoring 24 novels.

After taking a decade away because of the complications of Lyme Disease, Sylvie is back and happily writing again. Over the past 25 years, Sylvie has created engaging and uplifting romantic suspense novels. Today's world brings a lot of daily tension and uncertainties. So, Sylvie explores the labyrinth of relationships–from romantic to family to friendship. Her women's fiction allows the reader to experience adventures from the safety of home.

Her first Harlequin Intrigue, *One Texas Night*, was a 1999 Romantic Times nominee for Best First Category Romance and a finalist for a Booksellers Best Award. Her Silhouette Special Edition, *A Little Christmas Magic* was a 2001 Readers' Choice Award Finalist and a Waldenbooks bestseller. *Remembering Red Thunder* was a 2002 Romantic Times Nominee for Best Intrigue. She was a 2005, 2007 and 2008 Romantic Times nominee for Lifetime Achievement for Series Romantic Adventure. Twin Star Entertainment optioned *Ms. Longshot* as a possible TV movie.

For more details, visit https://sylviekurtz.com.

facebook.com/sylviekurtzauthor
instagram.com/sylviekurtzauthor

Milton Keynes UK
Ingram Content Group UK Ltd.
UKHW011050201123
432908UK00006BA/814